Eight Nights in December

Also by Keira Andrews

Contemporary

The Spy and the Mobster's Son
Honeymoon for One
Beyond the Sea
Ends of the Earth
Arctic Fire

Lifeguards of Barking Beach

Flash Rip
Free Wind

Holiday

The Christmas Deal
The Christmas Leap
The Christmas Veto
A Baby for Christmas
Only One Bed
Merry Cherry Christmas
Santa Daddy
In Case of Emergency
Eight Nights in December
If Only in My Dreams
Where the Lovelight Gleams
Gay Romance Holiday Collection

Sports

Kiss and Cry
Reading the Signs
Cold War
The Next Competitor
Love Match
Synchronicity (free read!)

Gay Amish Romance Series
A Forbidden Rumspringa
A Clean Break
A Way Home
A Very English Christmas

Valor Duology
Valor on the Move
Test of Valor
Complete Valor Duology

Historical

Kidnapped by the Pirate
Semper Fi
The Station
Voyageurs (free read!)

Paranormal

Kick at the Darkness Trilogy
Kick at the Darkness
Fight the Tide
Defy the Future

Fantasy

Barbarian Duet
Wed to the Barbarian
The Barbarian's Vow

Eight Nights in December

by Keira Andrews

Eight Nights in December
Written and published by Keira Andrews
Cover by Dar Albert

Copyright © 2017 by Keira Andrews
2ⁿᵈ Edition—revised and expanded
Earlier edition originally published by Loose Id in 2007
Print Edition

ISBN: 978-1-988260-76-1

Acknowledgements

Thank you to Anara Bella and Davina Jamison for their invaluable help with this reworked novella.

Chapter One

AS HE ROUNDED the staircase, Lucas McKenzie could already hear the pounding bass emanating from above. He cringed, knowing without a doubt it was coming from his room.

Well, Sam Kramer's room.

It was also technically Lucas's room, but Sam didn't let that stop him from doing exactly what he wanted to do, when he wanted to do it. As the star forward on Brookfield University's basketball team, Sam was used to getting his way, and Lucas didn't have the energy to argue most of the time.

Lucas trudged through the hallway, weaving around revelers celebrating the end of the December exam period. Everyone on the floor except Lucas was a senior, and although he knew some of them well enough to say hi to, it didn't go further than nods and smiles.

Heart already skipping at the thought of making small talk, he stepped over the drunken people sitting in his doorway and was greeted by a can of cold beer that bounced off his chest and rolled to a stop under the foot of his bed.

"Buddy!" *Everyone* was Sam's buddy. "School's out!" He whooped loudly, his muscled arms thrust over his head. Dark-haired Sam was tall and gorgeous; his chiseled features and sculpted muscles would be just as at home on a movie screen as they were on the basketball court.

Lucas ignored the acid flooding his belly and gave Sam a thumbs-up. "I'm totally stoked!" He'd learned early on in the semester that the best way to deal with Sam was to agree with everything he said. Besides, Lucas *should* be stoked. Exams were over, and what kind of college student didn't love partying and getting wasted?

From Lucas's estimation, he was apparently the only one.

"Grab a beer and party with us!"

Nodding and smiling, Lucas retrieved the beer from under his bed and popped the top after stashing his backpack in the closet—currently the only part of the small room that wasn't occupied by a fellow student. How were there so many people crammed in? Sweat prickled the back of his neck, and beer foamed out over his fingers. He gulped from the can.

A girl Lucas recognized as living down the hall was sprawled on his bed, sticking her tongue down the throat of a guy who looked old enough to be in his seventh or eighth year of college. Lucas thought wistfully of curling up under the covers and watching a movie on his laptop.

"Holidays are here!" Sam's proclamation was met with a loud cheer from the partygoers. Lucas kept the rictus smile on his face as he worked his way into the hallway, holding his can of beer aloft in a toast. He escaped back toward the stairwell, hoping that he wouldn't run into—

"Lucas!" Andrea Price materialized in front of him, grinning widely.

"Hey, Andrea. Um…" *Say something. This is the part where you say something.* "How's it going?"

"Great! I'm so glad exams are over. I can't wait to go home."

"Me either." Lucas found it easier to just lie. "Uh, well, enjoy the party."

Andrea touched his arm, her fingers light on his bicep. "I thought maybe we could hang out in my room downstairs." She looked up at him from under lashes thick with mascara.

Lucas groaned inwardly. Andrea was a fellow freshman and a beautiful girl—blonde and petite with a bright smile—but she just wasn't Lucas's type.

Not by a long shot.

He'd dated girls before, and he knew plenty of them found him attractive, but he wasn't sure why. He had no fashion sense to speak of, and although he was almost six feet, he didn't have bulging muscles like Sam and the other athletes. Yet the other day he'd overheard Andrea and her friend cooing about his "golden hair" and "sparkling green eyes—like emeralds!"

Vast exaggerations.

Unfortunately, he didn't find women attractive. At least, not in the way they found him. "Oh, I… Um, I've got a really bad headache. I'm just going to get some air." *Wait, would she think that was an invitation to go make out?* He blurted, "Alone."

Her face fell just a fraction before she smiled again. "Sure, I understand. Feel better. And merry Christmas if I don't see you again tonight."

"Right. You too. Um, thanks." He forced a bright, "Merry Christmas!" and winced inwardly at how awkward he sounded.

Leaving a disappointed Andrea in his wake, Lucas reached the stairwell and headed up one more flight to the roof. He would love to have her for a friend, but she seemed incapable of reading his signals, so he'd started avoiding her a few weeks earlier. He didn't want to lead her on or anything.

He'd briefly considered dating her so he could meet some other people, but he'd sworn when he left Michigan he'd stop pretending. Besides, it would be a dick move to date Andrea knowing he was using her. He had to come out and start being himself—whoever that was.

All signs point to being a total loser, he thought, cursing himself.

He was too chickenshit to join the campus gay association, so now he didn't date women *or* men. He told himself it would be his New Year's resolution to have the balls to join the club and at least *meet* some other LGBT people. Joining would make it official—still a bit of a scary prospect.

Frigid night air greeted him as he pushed the door open. A group of five or six people huddled together nearby, puffing away on cigarettes. Lucas nodded to them and walked to the other side of the roof, which was usually deserted. Leaning against the waist-high brick wall, he peered out, his breath clouding in front of his face.

He knew being antisocial wouldn't help him fit in at Brookfield, but parties made him stupidly anxious. What if he said the wrong thing? He was terrible at small talk. Plus, he looked like he was having a seizure when he danced, and he hated loud music and having so many people around.

Maybe he could just tell Andrea he was gay, and she would be cool with it and they could hang…

But what if she wasn't cool with it? His stomach clenched. What if she told everyone and Sam freaked out? Sam had been pissed enough to get stuck with a freshman roomie, and though he'd warmed to Lucas in his way, what if he was a homophobe? Lucas hadn't heard him using any slurs, but…

Thanks to his father's job in sales for Ford, Lucas had moved around a lot over the years and never made lasting friends. He'd hoped college would change that, but so far, not so much. He only had himself to blame, but the more he stressed about making friends the more he screwed it up and wanted to hide.

The bass from downstairs thudded through the soles of his sneakers, more bearable now at least. The campus spread out before him, lights twinkling merrily on the trees that lined the drives, winding their way around the stately old buildings.

It was December eighteenth, the last day of the fall semester. Lucas was fairly confident he'd done well on his last exam—*organic chemistry, ugh*—and he had hoped Sam's parents would have already picked him up. Sam lived in New York City, a few hours away from the tiny town in upstate New York that was home to Brookfield. Lucas wanted nothing more than to relax in his room and have an early night after being up late studying for the past two weeks.

Clearly he'd have to wait until tomorrow when the campus emptied to get some peace and quiet. Yet as much as he wanted some time to himself, Lucas knew that the next couple of weeks would be a little *too* quiet.

Tomorrow, all the students who hadn't already gone home would be taking off, leaving the campus a ghost town. The dorm advisor had told him he was the only one on his floor not going home for the holidays, and although he would be glad for the respite from the constant partying, spending Christmas completely alone was a depressing prospect. He enjoyed being by himself for the most part, but he was afraid loneliness would creep in and make itself a home.

He thought of his father and quickly took a gulp of beer to ward off the tightness in his throat. Some more smokers arrived, laughing gaily as they piled out onto the roof. Taking another swig of beer, Lucas stayed in the shadows.

"Uhhh."

Another sharp rap on the door echoed through the room, and Lucas forced himself to open his eyes, since it sounded like Sam wasn't yet able to form words. It didn't feel like Lucas had been sleeping long, but the light streaming through the window told a different story.

"Samuel, it's your mother." Her voice was soft yet firm on the other side of the door.

"Uhhh," Sam repeated, his head still buried under his duvet.

Lucas kicked empty beer cans under the bed and tried to cover up the evidence of the previous night's activities, shoving Sam's bong in a drawer. When he opened the door, he smiled brightly, not without some effort. "Mrs. Kramer? I'm Lucas."

"How nice to finally meet you." She extended her hand and shook his firmly, the jewels on her tasteful rings sparkling.

He stood aside as she swept into the room, surveying the piles of Sam's dirty clothes, books, and discarded pizza boxes. Mrs. Kramer looked to be in her early fifties, although Lucas couldn't be sure. Sam rarely mentioned his family; most of his conversations revolved around basketball, partying, and girls. Many, many girls.

Sam's mother was an average height, with dark brown, bobbed hair betraying no hint of gray. Her black skirt and camel-colored coat were crisply pressed.

"Samuel."

Sam groaned again unintelligibly.

Lucas smiled at Mrs. Kramer. "He's not really a morning person, but I guess you know that."

"Indeed I do." She marched the few steps over to Sam's bed, heels clicking on the tile floor. With a brisk motion, she yanked off the duvet. "Time to get up, young man."

Sam, clad only in his briefs, groaned again before rolling over onto his back and opening his eyes. "Mom, chill. I thought you were coming later."

"It is later. Almost noon."

Sam whined, "What's the rush?"

"Hanukkah starts tonight at sundown, which I've mentioned to you a number of times. So get up and get moving. It's a three-hour drive home, and I have things to do."

Grumbling under his breath, Sam stood and shuffled off to the bathroom down the hall, leaving Lucas and Mrs. Kramer alone. Lucas smiled. "I'd offer you a seat, but…"

Returning his smile, she perched on the side of Sam's bed. "This is fine." She glanced around the room one more time before focusing her attention on Lucas. "Are your parents coming today as well?"

Lucas hated this part. The creased faces and murmured apologies. The pity. "No, I don't have any family." He forced a smile. "But it's cool. I'll get the place to myself for a couple of weeks. It'll be great."

"No family? None at all?" Mrs. Kramer regarded him with a new interest that unnerved him a little.

"Well, I have some cousins in Texas, but I've never met them."

"What happened to your parents?"

Lucas blinked in surprise. Usually people beat around the bush for a while before getting to that question. "My mom died when I was little; my dad in September. Cancer."

"I'm so sorry to hear it." Her face pinched

in concern. "That must have been very difficult for you."

Difficult didn't really begin to cover it, but Lucas nodded. "Yeah."

"That's why you didn't start school until October. I remember Sam wasn't too happy to find out he'd be sharing a room after all. I told him he should have moved off campus, but he insisted on the dorm. I can only imagine that's due to the large number of young ladies living here." Her smile was wry.

"Yeah, Sam was *thrilled* to have me move in. But my profs were all really good about me starting late, especially since I'm only a freshman."

His father had insisted Lucas finally enroll in university for the fall, since the doctors hadn't expected him to make it to summer. When September rolled around, Lucas and his dad fought for days, Lucas refusing to leave his bedside while his father was adamant that at twenty, Lucas had already put off his future for long enough. Lucas won the battle, and had held his father's hand as he slipped away.

The school had been very accommodating about his late start, but now he was alone on a campus where everyone in his classes already made friends at the start of the year and, thanks to a housing shortage, his roommate was a senior jock. Lucas could move out—aside from the life insurance, his dad had left him a fair amount of money—but then he'd be even more isolated.

He cleared his throat, eager to move on to another topic. "So, Hanukkah starts tonight. That must be fun."

"Yes, it's a nice time of year. What will you do for Christmas?"

"Oh, just hang out or whatever. I'm not religious, so it's no big deal."

"Hmm." She stood and surveyed the room again. "Do you have a suitcase, or one of those duffel bags my son likes so much?"

"I'm sorry?" Lucas's duffel was somewhere at the bottom of his closet, and unless—

"Pack your bag, Lucas. You're going to spend the holidays with us."

"Oh, that's so nice of you, but I couldn't impose." Despite how lonely he might be over Christmas by himself, he was definitely looking forward to time away from Sam.

"You can, and you will. There's simply no way I'm leaving you here all alone."

"I really appreciate your concern, but I'll be fine. Really."

Sam returned, looking marginally more awake than when he left. His mother turned to him. "Samuel, Lucas will be coming to spend the holidays with us. Do you know where he keeps his overnight bag?"

Getting to his feet, Lucas was very tempted to tug on Mrs. Kramer's arm to get her to pay attention to what he was saying. "Thank you, but I'm not even Jewish. I don't want to intrude on your Hanukkah."

She waved him off. "Don't be ridiculous. You're more than welcome, and I'm not leaving you to..." She gazed around, nose wrinkling. "*This.*"

Yawning widely, Sam clapped him on the shoulder. "Dude, there's no point in arguing. Trust me."

Lucas opened his mouth to protest, but he couldn't think of a single good reason he should stay on campus alone for the holidays. Even if he had to put up with Sam, maybe he could do some sightseeing or something.

Half an hour later, Lucas found himself in the back of the Kramer family SUV, heading toward New York City as the first snowflakes of the season drifted down.

Chapter Two

A S THEY CROSSED the bridge to Staten Island, Lucas peered out the window as the city passed by. Sam snored lightly in the front seat, and Mrs. Kramer listened to a talk radio station that Lucas had tuned out near Poughkeepsie.

"Have you ever been to the city before?" Mrs. Kramer asked. Her voice jolted Lucas from his reverie.

"No, this is my first time."

"We'll have to show you around."

"Oh, you don't have to do that." Lucas already felt awkward enough.

"I insist. I'm sure Sam would be more than happy to take you into Manhattan. There's a wonderful Degas exhibit at the Frick."

Lucas realized the best way to deal with Mrs. Kramer was the same way he dealt with

Sam: He nodded and smiled. "Thanks, that sounds great." Of course, the idea of Sam voluntarily going anywhere that didn't serve beer seemed highly unlikely.

They were only on the island for ten minutes before they pulled into the driveway of a large, two-story brick home. The lawn and shrubs were as neatly manicured as Mrs. Kramer, and large picture windows glowed with soft lights in the overcast afternoon.

"What a beautiful home you have."

Sam roused from his slumber and grunted. Mrs. Kramer smiled widely in the rearview mirror, her lipstick still somehow untouched despite the cup of coffee she'd had. "Thank you, dear."

Inside, a man Lucas assumed to be Sam's father shuffled into the foyer to greet them. He was tall, thin, and balding, with glasses propped on his head. He looked as if he'd just woken from a nap. "Hello, son. Good drive home?" He pulled Sam into a hug.

"Hey, Dad. Yeah, sure."

"He slept the whole way as usual, Benjamin. Just like you would have done."

Mr. Kramer shrugged sheepishly. "Like father, like son, I suppose." He suddenly noticed Lucas hovering just inside the door, holding his duffel bag. "And who's this?"

Mrs. Kramer ushered Lucas forward with a gentle hand on his arm. "If you'd check your phone for messages, you would know that this is Sam's roommate, Lucas. He's going to spend the holidays with us."

After blinking in surprise, Mr. Kramer smiled broadly, shaking Lucas's hand firmly. "Welcome! It's good to meet you."

"Thanks, nice to meet you too." Lucas peered around at what he could see of the tastefully decorated home. The living room featured dark redwood, accented with rich reds and yellows. He glimpsed the kitchen at the end of the front hall and saw more redwood cupboards and stainless steel appliances.

"Sam's room is still a disgusting mess from Thanksgiving." Mrs. Kramer glared at Sam as he opened his mouth. "I told you I'm not your maid anymore." Glancing at her delicate gold watch, she pressed her lips together. "I've got to get organized in the kitchen; everyone will be here before we know it. Nathaniel has the extra bed in his room, so Lucas can stay there."

Lucas followed Sam up a plush staircase off to the right. "Lucky you, you get to crash with my geeky little brother."

"Are you sure he won't mind?" Lucas

certainly wouldn't be happy, and he had to admit the thought of rooming with a kid wasn't his idea of a good time. Sam was bad enough.

"Who cares? What Mom says goes." At the top of the stairs, Sam pounded on the first door on the left. "Yo, loser! Open up." With that, he continued down the hall, which was decorated in muted tones of green and brown.

"Wait, aren't you going to introduce us?"

"Dude, I've gotta piss." With that, Sam disappeared into another doorway, kicking the door shut behind him.

After waiting a good twenty seconds without a response, Lucas knocked tentatively. He didn't hear any movement inside, so after another half minute, he knocked a little louder. This time he heard what sounded like a curse, followed by a barked, "What?"

Lucas slowly poked his head in. The large bedroom had two twin beds jutting out from the left-hand wall, and Sam's brother sat at a desk straight ahead against the window side of the room. Lucas saw immediately that he wasn't a little kid at all. From the back, he looked at least Lucas's age, with short, wavy chestnut hair.

"I'm reading, Sam."

"Um, I'm sorry to bother you." Lucas

stood in the doorway awkwardly, not sure how to proceed.

Nathaniel spun in his seat. "Who are you?" He stared with big eyes through a pair of black-framed glasses, his soft features making him more pretty than handsome.

"I'm Sam's roommate. From college. I guess I'm going to be your roommate for the holidays." He glanced around the neat room, covered in childish wallpaper depicting sailboats and anchors. In the center of each wall was a large, framed black-and-white photograph. The stark and beautiful pictures of mountains and trees seemed out of place.

Nathaniel took this in before he smiled ruefully. "Clearly this was my mother's doing."

"How'd you guess?" Lucas smiled back. "Look man, I'm sorry. I wouldn't be too happy if I were you."

He shrugged. "It's cool."

"Thanks. I'm Lucas, by the way." He dropped his bag and walked to the desk, putting his hand out.

Nathaniel stood, and Lucas could see they were almost the same height, Nathaniel perhaps an inch or two shorter. He regarded Lucas for a long moment before taking his hand. "Call me Nate."

Butterflies flapped in Lucas's stomach, and he said too loudly, "Okay, Nate!" He cleared his throat, pulling his hand away. "Um. I mean, cool. Or whatever." He glanced around again. "You like boats?"

Nate smirked. "Not for about ten years. I need to update my room, I know." He watched Lucas for a few moments, his eyes flicking down and then back up to Lucas's face. Then he reached out and squeezed Lucas's shoulder, sending sparks down his arm. "Make yourself at home, okay?"

Lucas could only nod before turning to grab his bag. Sam's little brother was *hot*. He scolded himself sternly. *Do not crush on him. Don't be lame. Don't make sharing a room weird!*

When he turned back, Nate was bending over his desk, tapping at his laptop. His firm, denim-clad ass was on full display, and Lucas could barely tear his gaze away. Sam was such a doofus that Lucas wasn't attracted to him at all despite his good looks. He was a little too muscle-bound anyway. But Nate was long and lean, his skinny jeans hugging his thighs…

Nate glanced over his shoulder, pushing his glasses up his nose. "Do you need anything?"

Hell yes. Lucas managed to squeak out,

"No!" and busied himself with rooting through his duffel bag.

The *need* had been simmering for years now, but he'd been too afraid to hook up with another guy. Lucas ordered himself to get a grip and make sure he didn't embarrass himself. Maybe he should have stayed alone in the dorm after all.

Yet he couldn't help sneaking peeks at Nate, who seemed oblivious as he pecked at his computer, still leaning over the desk.

There was no harm in looking, right?

LUCAS SMOOTHED DOWN his shirt with the palm of his hand and wished again that he'd thought to ask Mrs. Kramer for an iron. The black button-down was the only good shirt he owned, and after being squashed in his bag for a few hours, it was a little worse for wear.

He leaned against the doorframe between the living and dining rooms, watching as Sam's relatives chatted happily. There were grandparents, aunts, uncles, and cousins. Fourteen people in all. They'd been very friendly when he was introduced, but Lucas couldn't help but feel out of his element. He hadn't been to many family gatherings, and never any Jewish celebrations.

"All right, time to light the menorah!" Mrs. Kramer clapped her hands once for attention. "Samuel, why don't you do the honors and read the blessings?"

Sam didn't look too excited, but he dutifully stepped up to the ornate candleholder in the front window. From the elevated candle in the center, two wings of four candles curved down gracefully to the left and right. After a moment, Sam spoke in what Lucas assumed was Hebrew.

Almost all of the guests recited the blessing along with Sam. Two more blessings followed, and Lucas wondered if he should bow his head. He glanced around the room and found Nate watching him from the other side. Cheeks going hot, Lucas focused on Sam as he lit the center candle on the menorah, followed by the one farthest to the right.

"Nathaniel, come and say the *Hanerot Halalu*. Stop hiding in the back." Mrs. Kramer extended her hand, and Nate came forward.

Taking a small book from his mother, he straightened his glasses and began reading quietly. His voice was soft and melodious in contrast to Sam's, and Lucas could hardly believe they were related at all, let alone brothers.

When Nate was finished, Mr. Kramer burst into song, everyone else following suit. Lucas couldn't understand the lyrics, and as the verses went on, it seemed like only the older people knew all the words. After the song ended, Mrs. Kramer brought out trays filled with what looked like lightly powdered doughnuts without holes.

"Hands down, the best part of Hanukkah." A pretty young woman with long, reddish hair smiled eagerly at Lucas, a tray in her hand. "Try one."

Lucas returned her smile and picked up a doughnut. "Thanks. Um, uh…" He managed to ask, "What's your name?"

"I'm Rachel. Sam and Nate are my cousins. You're Lucas, right?" She beamed at him.

"I am." Lucas glanced at Nate, alone across the room, thumbing through the prayer book. "So what's Nate like?" He hoped his tone was casual.

"Nate? He's always been quiet. He's twenty-one now, but he's still never had a girlfriend. Always too busy studying and taking pictures. I don't know; he's weird." Shame flickered across her face. "I mean, I love him, of course! He's a really good guy."

He nodded. "Oh, of course." Mrs. Kramer

walked by, apparently in the middle of an argument with an elderly man.

Rachel rolled her eyes. "Don't mind them. Papa still thinks we should observe the Sabbath every Friday. That would mean going to synagogue and not cooking anything or using cars to get home. No electricity at all. It's just not practical."

"Does he follow the rules every week?"

"Yes, but he and Bubbe—our grandmother—are the only observant ones in the family." Rachel leaned in and lowered her voice. "Except if there's a Mets game on a Friday. Then all bets are off."

Laughing, Lucas took a bite of his doughnut, and a divine sweetness filled his mouth. "Wow, you're right. That's delicious. I didn't know you guys had holiday doughnuts."

Laughing, she said, "*Sufganiyot*, but yeah, that's basically what they are."

"And you eat them before dinner?"

"In our family we eat them before and after. Sometimes during," Nate said, appearing beside Lucas and reaching out to the tray.

Lucas laughed. "Beats turkey, that's for sure." Not that he and his father ever had a traditional Christmas. They'd made their own tradition: pizza, junk food, and football on TV. His dad had loved football, and even though Lucas didn't, he never complained.

He remembered their last Christmas, when his dad couldn't keep anything down thanks to the never-ending chemo. All his thick, dark hair was gone, his face puffy and body frail. He'd fallen asleep in his armchair at halftime, but Lucas had kept the game on, just in case his dad woke up.

Nate frowned. "Are you okay?"

"Huh? Oh yeah." Lucas nodded vigorously and took a huge bite of doughnut.

"Rachel, I think my mom needs you in the kitchen," Nate said.

As she scurried off, Lucas swallowed, blinking rapidly as he looked at the floor. He was going to make a fool of himself if he didn't get it together. After a calming breath, he took another bite of his doughnut and tried to act normal. "So, you guys eat like this for eight nights in a row?"

Nate smiled softly. "No, we just have a big dinner on the first night and once again before it's over, depending on everyone's schedules. We light the menorah every night, but that's about it. Hanukkah's actually not that big a deal. It's not a high holiday like Yom Kippur or Rosh Hashanah."

Another tray went by, and they both grabbed another sweet treat. Lucas knew his dad would want him to move on and be happy, and he'd worried so much about leaving Lucas alone. Lucas had promised to make friends, and since he'd failed utterly so far at school, maybe he could start with Nate. He asked, "What other Jewish delicacies await me tonight?"

"You like potatoes?"

"Does anyone *not* like potatoes?"

Nate seemed to ponder the question seriously. "No one I can think of." He added, "Tonight the potatoes will be in pancake form. *Latkes.*"

"I really hope there isn't maple syrup involved."

As Nate grinned, a dimple appeared in his left cheek, and Lucas felt a flutter in the pit of his stomach. He'd made Nate laugh! This was going okay. He wasn't saying anything stupid. Not yet, anyway.

He reminded himself again that the last thing he needed was to crush on his roommate's brother. The brother he was sharing a room with for the next two weeks. He was going to make a friend, and that was all.

Mrs. Kramer dashed by, insisting that Lucas eat the last sufganiyot on her tray. He gratefully obeyed and stuffed it in his mouth.

"It's time to sit down." Nate's hand was

warm on Lucas's shoulder, and there was that tingle again. He nodded and followed him into the dining room, hoping his cheeks weren't too bright.

LUCAS WOKE TO pressure on his bladder and the faint sound of running water that had permeated his consciousness. He opened his eyes reluctantly and took in the early morning gloom. According to his phone it was after eight, but evidently it would be another gray, cloudy day.

He sat up and surveyed the room. Nate's bed beside him, closest to the windows, was empty. Across the way, an extra wardrobe stood in the corner beside the bathroom, and light shone through the half-open bathroom door, the water running in the shower.

Lucas couldn't wait to pee. He got up to venture into the hall to find another toilet, but hesitated as he glanced back at the half-open door. Without really knowing what he was doing, he tiptoed toward it. A couple of feet away he stopped suddenly, breath frozen in his chest.

Through the doorway he could spy the large mirror over the white sink. Reflected in it was Nate, who Lucas could see quite clearly through a completely transparent shower curtain. Nate's head tipped back under the water as his hands soaped his body.

A body that was more toned and defined than Lucas would ever have guessed.

Lucas forced a breath into his lungs as his pulse thrummed. With a start, he realized he was hard—not unusual first thing in the morning—and he clenched his fist to avoid touching himself.

Nate began stroking himself lazily as if on cue. He leaned a shoulder against the white tiles, and his eyes closed as he worked his hand up and down his shaft. He tugged a few times, and Lucas whimpered with need.

The water sluiced down Nate's firm, long body, steam rising as he worked himself. Lucas moved a step closer, squinting at the image in the mirror to get a better look. With his other hand, Nate fondled his balls, and his strokes increased in tempo.

Lucas wasn't sure when it happened, but his own hand was down his pajamas, fist tight around his cock and moving like a jackhammer. The mirror in the bathroom was fogging, and Lucas knew he couldn't risk getting any closer. He heard Nate's muffled moan, and the sound was enough to put Lucas over the edge as he emptied, the rush of pleasure practically knocking him over.

There was a soft thud as he caught himself on the wall, and in the fogged mirror he thought he saw Nate's head turn his way.

Shit! How much can he see without his glasses?

Lucas stumbled backward and dove onto his bed, pulling the covers up and flipping on his side toward the door.

With his eyes jammed shut, he tried to catch his breath and keep still. A minute later, he heard Nate pad into the room. Lucas feigned sleep as Nate dressed, ignoring the fact that now he really, *really* had to pee.

When Nate finally left the room, closing the door gently behind him, Lucas waited thirty seconds and then hurried into the bathroom to relieve himself. His pajamas were a sticky mess. He couldn't exactly hang them to dry, so he spread them out under his duvet after a quick rinse, knowing he might have to sleep in a damp bed that night.

He needed to get a grip, and fast. As he pulled on jeans and buttoned up a plaid shirt, he muttered to himself, "Just not a grip on my dick this time."

Downstairs, Nate and his father talked quietly at the kitchen table, sipping coffee.

Wearing jeans and an unzipped purple hoodie, Nate got up and poured Lucas a steaming mug, their fingers brushing when he handed it over. Lucas stammered out his thanks. Nate seemed totally normal and went back to his conversation with his dad, taking off his glasses and polishing the lenses with his gray T-shirt.

Soon Lucas was embroiled in a discussion with Mr. Kramer about Sam's many achievements in basketball. As Mr. Kramer waxed poetic on a game-winning layup Sam had made, Lucas pondered what Rachel had said about Nate's lack of girlfriend.

It didn't mean anything. Probably Nate dated around like Sam and didn't tell his family about it. It didn't mean he was gay or bi or anything. Lucas was gay, and he'd never even had the courage to kiss a guy. Nate not having a girlfriend proved nothing.

Every time Lucas glanced at Nate across the kitchen table, his temperature rose with a rush of desire. God, he wanted him, and now they'd be in close quarters for days on end. Looking, but not touching.

It was going to be a very, very long holiday.

Chapter Three

LUCAS SPENT THE afternoon with Sam and his father in the den, watching football on a big-screen TV that made Lucas practically drool. Nate had disappeared into his room after lunch, and Lucas tried not to obsess about what he was doing.

It was just after five when Mrs. Kramer told them it was time to light the menorah. Sam groaned, and Lucas could have sworn Mr. Kramer did too, but they obediently headed to the front room.

Nate was already there, the matches in hand. As Lucas watched Nate, he couldn't help but remember how Nate had looked naked and wet and jerking himself, and he mentally slapped himself with the reminder that this was a religious ceremony.

Nate seemed to only recite two blessings before lighting the middle candle and two on the right, doing the outer candle last. Lucas thought there had been three blessings the night before, but couldn't be sure. As if he could read Lucas's mind, Nate said, "There are only three blessings on the first night, and we don't bother with the prayer and song when it's just us."

"Can we get back to the game now?" Sam looked at his mother.

Her hands found her hips and she good-naturedly said, "You know this is supposed to be a time for family, not for TV."

"Sweetheart, it's the fourth quarter." Mr. Kramer gave his wife a beseeching smile.

With a laugh, she shooed them out, her husband kissing her soundly on his way. "Go on, Lucas. I'll be in with dinner in a little while."

"Do you want any help? I don't really care that much about football." Nate was already at the foot of the stairs, and Lucas willed him to turn around and stay.

Nate smirked. "Don't care about sports? That's sacrilege in this house." Then he was gone, his steps fading as he went back upstairs.

Sam's voice bellowed from the den. "Dude, you've got to see this play! Come on, you're missing it!"

With a smile for Mrs. Kramer, Lucas reluctantly returned.

AFTER A DINNER of leftovers on TV trays, Lucas and the Kramers watched an action movie about an alien invasion on Netflix. Nate had come down for dinner, but disappeared back up to his room halfway through the movie. Lucas fidgeted in the stuffed armchair in the corner of the plush, dark den. What was Nate doing up there? Not that it was any of Lucas's business.

You already invaded the guy's space without warning. Give him his alone time.

The nanosecond the movie credits appeared onscreen, Lucas yawned widely and said goodnight. Mrs. Kramer gave him a plate of sufganiyot to take up to Nate, saying, "He's always hiding away up there. He doesn't eat enough."

Lucas knocked softly on Nate's closed bedroom door, waiting a few moments before opening it. To his surprise, Nate wasn't in the darkened room, and the bathroom appeared empty. The space around the closet door glowed with a strange reddish light, and Lucas blinked at it, thinking of the 10-foot, red-eyed aliens from the movie. After a moment of debate, he approached and knocked.

"Hold on," Nate called.

"Um, okay." Lucas stood there with the plate of doughnuts, wondering what on earth could be going on inside.

Two long minutes later, Nate opened the door and Lucas flooded with embarrassment for not figuring out that the red light was indicative of a darkroom. *Duh. I'm such a loser.*

The walk-in closet had been fashioned into a working space with a counter running around the perimeter holding trays of developing liquid. A clothesline ran across the back of the closet, large photographs pinned to it.

"You're a photographer?"

Nate chuckled, but not in a dickish way. "You clearly have a future as a detective."

Face hot, Lucas shuffled his feet, laughing awkwardly. "Clearly." He suddenly remembered the plate in his hand. "Here. Your mom thinks you need to eat more. I can just leave them."

"You wanna come in? I've just got to develop a couple more shots."

Lucas nodded and pulled the door shut behind him. Enclosed in the small space with

Nate, his pulse raced. In the soft red glow, Nate looked better than ever, and Lucas fought the urge to reach out and touch him.

He cleared his throat and attempted to clear his mind. "I guess this explains why you keep your clothes in that separate wardrobe thingy."

"Yeah, Mom was overjoyed when I made this a darkroom, as I'm sure you can imagine." He glanced over his shoulder as he splashed some fluid into one of the trays. "You ever develop a picture before?"

"Uh-uh." Lucas had been examining what looked to be a couple of little moles on the back of Nate's neck and didn't feel capable of complete sentences. Lucas had removed the hoodie, and his back flexed through the white tee.

"I'll show you."

As Nate went through the steps, Lucas tried to pay attention. At one point, Nate handed him a pair of rubber-tipped tongs, and Lucas dutifully plucked out a developed photo and hung it on the line. They worked in companionable silence, and Lucas found he enjoyed watching the photographs come to life. They were all black-and-white cityscapes, and a frisson of excitement zipped through him. He'd finally get a chance to see New

York for himself in the days to come.

Maybe Nate could show me around.

"You took all of these?" Lucas admired the clean lines and unique angles of the photos.

Nate waved his hand dismissively. "Yeah, I'm just messing around."

"I'd like to see what you can do when you're taking it seriously because these are amazing."

"It's nice of you to say so." Nate wiped his hands on a towel and plucked a doughnut from the plate Lucas had left on the counter. "We just need to wait now before we open the door."

Nate didn't seem comfortable with praise, so Lucas stopped talking and took his own doughnut, relishing the sweet, fruity flavor. He couldn't understand why Nate trivialized his talent. Lucas was no expert, but he found the photographs beautiful, particularly one taken from a low angle of a cathedral, a balloon floating away in the corner. He wondered what color the balloon had been but didn't ask. It was probably a stupid question.

They ate in silence, and Lucas noticed a blob of jelly filling on the corner of Nate's mouth. Before he could think, he reached out, swiping at it with his finger. Their eyes locked, and Lucas froze, his hand still at Nate's mouth.

Oh God, what was he doing?

He stayed in place, not breathing as he and Nate stared at each other in the muted red light. Before Lucas could process what was happening, Nate's tongue curled out and licked the jelly from his finger. A jolt of desire shot right to Lucas's balls, and he swallowed thickly, his throat suddenly dry.

Then Nate turned his head just a bit and sucked Lucas's finger into his mouth, his gaze behind his glasses locked on Lucas's face.

As Lucas moaned low in his throat, heart pounding, Nate yanked him close, and they were kissing. Lucas's head swam from the explosion of sensations.

They. Were. *Kissing.*

He was actually kissing another man. He'd dreamed of it, and somehow it was happening. He opened his mouth, and Nate's tongue dived in, probing and stroking as his hands ran over Lucas's back, down to his ass.

Quiet, allegedly mild-mannered Nathaniel Kramer was grabbing his ass.

Head swimming, Lucas kissed Nate back, his body alive in a way it had never been while kissing a girl. The scratch of Nate's stubble, his musky scent, his strong body hauling

Lucas close—everything about him was so *male.*

I really am gay! I'm kissing a guy!

Giddy and burning with lust at the same time, Lucas explored Nate's mouth, their kisses sweet from the doughnuts.

They both gasped for air, and Lucas realized his jeans were now undone as Nate sank to his knees. "What are you…?"

As Nate grinned wickedly and took Lucas in his mouth, all intelligent thought fled. Lucas leaned back against the counter, his hands searching for purchase as he moaned at the wet heat of Nate's mouth. His right hand slid into one of the developing trays, liquid splashing as Nate sucked him into his throat.

Lucas's whole body vibrated. Nate's tongue was doing things he'd never imagined possible, and it certainly hadn't felt like this when Paige Gallner had awkwardly sucked him off on prom night.

It felt like his cock was pulsing in time with his heart, all his nerve endings on fire. Nate pushed up Lucas's plaid shirt with one hand, fingers skimming over Lucas's belly and up to his nipples.

"Oh!" Lucas cried out, then slapped his own hand over his mouth.

Nate pulled off and said, "Yeah, keep it

down, okay?"

"I'm sorry."

"It's okay." Nate caressed Lucas's belly, making him squirm, watching him. "Have you done this before?"

"I… No. Not really. A girl did this to me once, but it wasn't anything like this."

Lazily stroking Lucas's shaft, Nate waggled his eyebrows above his glasses. "Well, you're in good hands now."

"Literally. I never thought—Sam said you're a geek, but you're not at all."

Nate dipped his fingers behind Lucas's balls, pressing the sensitive skin there. He grinned as Lucas trembled and bucked his hips. "Geeks can be good at fucking. I promise."

Lucas could only moan, his breath hitching.

After licking along the bottom of Lucas's cock, Nate asked, "You like guys? You like this?"

"Uh-huh." He nodded jerkily. "Doesn't it seem like I do?"

Nate grinned. "Yes, but I just wanted to make sure." His smile faded, and he teased the tip of Lucas's cut dick before asking, "Want to come in my mouth?"

He could only whimper and nod, and

Nate sucked him almost to the root, his cheeks hollowing. Lucas quivered, his knees shaking as Nate cradled his balls with his other hand. He tipped over the edge, red-tinged stars exploding in his vision as he came and Nate swallowed.

Nate held Lucas up with strong hands on his hips, standing a few moments later. He swiped his mouth with the back of his hand and straightened his glasses. Then casually unzipped his jeans and shoved them down his hips before pulling out his cock. It was cut and thick, the tip gleaming in the red light.

"Uh…" Lucas still couldn't seem to form a sentence, which made Nate smile as he began jerking himself off. Lucas watched, wide-eyed. "Can I?"

Nate dropped his hand. "Be my guest."

So many times Lucas had imagined what it would be like to touch another guy's dick. He'd done it as a kid once with a schoolmate, but that had only been mutual curiosity. They'd been too young to really know what they were doing, and had only poked and goofed around.

This was a man's cock Lucas was wrapping his hand around. It throbbed hot against his palm, and he twisted his hand to get a good angle as he stroked. His fingers brushed wiry hair at the base, and Nate's puffs of breath tickled Lucas's face as he leaned closer, his hand slipping around Lucas's shoulder, holding on.

"That's it. Just do it like you'd do to yourself."

Lucas lifted his hand to spit into his palm a couple of times, and Nate took his wrist, bending his head to lick Lucas's hand, spitting into it himself. Lucas's balls tingled, his dick twitching already at the rough sensation of Nate's tongue.

When Lucas stroked Nate again, Nate groaned, his hand sliding farther around Lucas's shoulder, fingers reaching up to tug at the short hair at the back of Lucas's neck.

I'm really doing this. I'm touching his dick. I'm jerking him off!

Of course his stupid brain felt the need to blurt, "So, you're gay too?"

Nate raised his eyebrows, smiling as he breathed hard, arching his hips into Lucas's hand. "Detective material for sure."

"Did you know I was gay as well?"

"I hoped you were when you walked into my room. You're so fucking hot. But I *knew* when you watched me jerk off in the shower."

Blood rushing to his cheeks, glad the red

light of the darkroom would conceal it, Lucas squeaked. His rhythm on Nate's cock stuttered. "You saw me? I'm sorry. I shouldn't have—I didn't—"

"Shh." Nate caught Lucas's mouth in a kiss, and Lucas moaned as he realized the musky salt he was tasting amid the lingering hint of sugar was his own cum. Nate leaned back, eyes twinkling. "I left the door open on purpose. I figured if you fell into my trap, this Hanukkah could be a lot more fun than the usual games of dreidel."

"I..." Lucas's mind spun. Nate's other words registered belatedly. "You think I'm hot?"

Nate's brow furrowed. "Uh, *yeah*. Have you looked in a mirror?" He thrust his hips against Lucas's hand. "You get me really hard."

"Uh, thank you?" Blood rushed in Lucas's ears. This had to be a dream.

Laughing softly, Nate kissed him again, just a gentle press of lips. "You're welcome. What do you say we have some fun this holiday?"

"Okay." Breathless, Lucas nodded. "Yes."

Nate arched an eyebrow over the black rim of his glasses. "Now how about you make me come?"

Lucas had never been happier to oblige a request in his life.

Chapter Four

"LOOK AT THIS fog—sticking around all day! There's a gorgeous view from this bridge, but I'm afraid the weather's not cooperating."

Lucas spoke up from the backseat. "Don't worry, Mrs. Kramer. I'm sure I'll see the view another day."

"You simply must. Perhaps you can come back into the city on the ferry. You'll get a good look at the Statue of Liberty too. I'm afraid I don't like heights, or I'd take you up the Empire State Building myself when there's better visibility." She glanced in the rearview mirror. "Sam, you'll take Lucas back tomorrow?"

"I've got stuff to do with my friends. I already spent a whole day at a stupid museum with you guys. Why did I have to come?"

"*Samuel.*"

The truth was, Lucas couldn't have cared less about seeing the city anymore. What he cared about was that Nate had been an arm's length away from him all day and he couldn't touch him. Nate had taken the front seat after a heated debate with Sam, and he was tantalizingly close, yet out of reach. Lucas's leg jiggled, and he noted the traffic with impatience. He just wanted to be back in Nate's room.

Back in his bed.

Well, he hadn't slept there or anything. After they'd made out again and Nate had given Lucas another mind-bending blow job, they'd slept in their separate beds. Lucas knew it was stupid to sleep together in a tiny twin bed when Nate's parents could walk in at any time, but he still wanted to. When he'd woken that morning, Nate was already downstairs, and they'd been on the go all day.

"Mom, I've got plans!" Sam whined.

Lucas cleared this throat. "You know, I can just come back by myself."

"I can take him." Nate's voice was so quiet, Lucas barely heard him.

"Will you, darling? I thought you'd be busy with your little hobby. So many hours you spend locked up in that closet."

It occurred to Lucas that he didn't know if

the Kramers knew Nate was gay. Was he in the closet in that regard as well? Lucas could hardly blame him. He'd only come out to his dad near the end. He hadn't wanted to upset him, but the thought of never telling him the truth was unbearable.

Thinking of how his father had kissed his forehead and told him he loved him just as he was, Lucas's eyes burned. He pushed away the memories before he burst into tears and freaked everyone out.

"It's not a problem." Lucas thought he could detect an edge to Nate's voice now.

"Yeah, because King Geek doesn't have any friends." Sam cackled.

"*Samuel.* Your brother has lots of friends at NYU. He's in the law society, after all."

"Just no friends I'd introduce to you, asswipe," Nate added.

Lucas turned his head to the window as Nate and Sam continued bickering. There was something oddly reassuring about it, and the way Mrs. Kramer interjected every so often. The sense of familiarity with each other left him yearning.

After what seemed like an eternity, they were home. Lucas wanted nothing more than to escape to Nate's room and spend the whole night there, but he had to make more small talk and sit through another dinner.

First they gathered in the living room and lit the candles on the menorah, adding another to the right-hand side, but lighting them in order from the middle. Mr. Kramer recited the blessings beforehand, and Lucas tried to listen and not think about how he wanted to lick Nate's Adam's apple. Trying to be sociable, he asked, "What's the story behind Hanukkah? Something about oil, right?"

Mr. Kramer grinned. "Well, there's an old joke that every Jewish holiday boils down to: They tried to kill us; they didn't—let's eat."

Mrs. Kramer jumped in. "After the Maccabees reclaimed the Temple in Jerusalem from their enemies, there was only enough oil to light the eternal flame for one day. However, the oil lasted for eight nights."

"A miracle." Mr. Kramer clapped his hands together. "Okay, let's eat."

At the dinner table, Lucas pushed Thai takeout around on his plate, and afterwards he tried to concentrate on the game of Rummikub Mr. Kramer suggested, but ended up with the most tiles every time. Although Nate had retreated to his room, Lucas couldn't think of a good reason to go to bed at eight o'clock.

When he finally escaped an hour later, he thought he might explode with pent-up desire and frustration. He practically ran up the stairs and burst into Nate's room without knocking. Nate, lying on his bed, looked up from the book he was reading, the lamplight glinting off his glasses.

"Good game?"

"Not really; I kept getting stuck with high numbers I couldn't get rid of."

"Too bad." Nate yawned widely. "I was just about to go to sleep. So if you want to read or anything, can you use that little lamp on your side?"

Lucas was speechless for a moment. "Yeah. Sure." That was it? Nate was going to *sleep*? Shame and embarrassment flooded Lucas like a hot, prickly tide. He wished he could be anywhere else. Apparently Nate wasn't interested in him at all anymore.

Standing, Nate pulled his sweater over his head, stretching his arms up high and yawning again. He unzipped his khakis and stepped out of them before carefully folding his clothes and placing them on his desk chair, clad only in his boxers. Lucas, still standing dumbly, watched.

Nate strolled back to his bed and stretched out. He glanced over at Lucas and burst out laughing. "Oh man, I should take a picture of your face right now."

Son of a… "This is your idea of a joke?"

As Nate patted the mattress beside him, Lucas didn't know whether to kiss him or kill him, but when he had Nate's warm skin under his palms, he knew it would be the former. He covered Nate's body with his own as their mouths met.

They kissed for minutes or maybe hours, until Nate propped himself up on his elbows and took a breather. "You took forever to get up here. It was torture today not being able to touch you. That's why I insisted I sit in the front. Man, I thought you were going to jump me at the dinner table. Good thing my family's so clueless."

"So they don't know you're gay?"

"Nope. Like I said—clueless."

Lucas wondered why Nate didn't tell them, but as he rubbed against Nate, his dick hard in his jeans, he figured he'd ask another time. "So you were playing hard to get just now?"

"Of course." Nate grinned, displaying his dimple and sending another rush of blood right to Lucas's cock.

"I thought maybe… I thought you weren't interested anymore." Lucas glanced away. Why did he say that out loud?

"Shit, I'm sorry. I shouldn't play games with a virgin."

He cringed. *I'm so lame.* "A girl blew me after prom. Does that count?"

"If you want it to." Nate ran his hands over Lucas's back down to his ass.

"Not really. It was super awkward. It just felt…wrong, you know? Not like with you." Clearly Nate was experienced, considering the things he could do with his tongue. "How many people have you been with?"

"No *people.* Just guys." He looked thoughtful for a moment. "I don't know. My fair share. I went to a gay bar during frosh week, and the rest, as they say, is history."

Wow. Nate had been with men. *Multiple* men.

"Don't worry. I get tested regularly, and I'm careful."

Lucas had been wondering how to bring that up. "So you've dated a lot of guys?"

Nate laughed. "Dated? Not really. I guess I've kind of dated a few. Well, I had sex with them more than once." He peered closely at Lucas, his brown eyes intense behind his square-ish glasses. "Just so you know, I'm not looking for a boyfriend."

"Oh. Why not?" Lucas hoped he didn't

sound as needy as he felt. He was lying on top of the guy and it seemed so *intimate*.

It's just fooling around. Go with it. Don't be a loser for once.

"I can't exactly bring home a nice boy to Mom and Dad. It's easier this way. Besides, I'm not good at that stuff." He smiled. "I like sex. I'm *good* at sex. Why complicate it?"

"But—"

Nate leaned up and caught Lucas's bottom lip between his teeth. "Let's stop talking," he whispered.

They kissed again, and Lucas explored Nate's body. He'd never been able to handle another man so freely, and he reveled in touching and tasting. He sucked one of Nate's nipples into his mouth, delighting in the soft moan that escaped Nate's lips. As he moved lower, his heart pounded in excitement.

He was really going to do it.

He'd thought about it a million times and wondered what it would be like to suck a dick: how it would taste, how it would feel, what it would smell like. He nuzzled the trail of hair that led down from Nate's belly button, and Nate lifted his hips as Luke pulled off his boxers.

Lucas was still in his jeans and green Henley, and Nate's nudity fired his blood.

Especially when he spread his legs wide, unashamed, his cock flushed, standing up from the trimmed patch of hair. He watched Lucas patiently, keeping his hands at his sides.

Taking Nate's cock tentatively, Lucas rubbed it on his cheek, his chin, his lips. He wrapped his hand around Nate's shaft, exploring and working up his nerve. His pulse raced, stomach clenching. It must have shown on his face, because Nate stroked his hair gently and said, "You don't have to."

Screw that. He wanted to. More than that—he'd explode if he didn't. With a deep breath, he swallowed the head of Nate's cock, wrapping his lips around him as far as he could. The shaft was heavy and hot in his mouth, and saliva dripped down his chin. Lucas moved his head up and down, sucking and licking like he was enjoying a popsicle on a hot summer's day.

A dick popsicle. A dicksicle, even.

Slurping, loving the musky, slightly bitter tang, he remembered what Nate had done, and fisted the base of Nate's shaft as he sucked what he could into his mouth. He traced his tongue up the ridge on the back, and Nate moaned, making Lucas even harder in his jeans. He humped the mattress between Nate's spread legs to get some friction on his straining dick.

Nate's fingers tangled in Lucas's hair, and he muttered under his breath. "That's it. Like that. You're doing so good."

Lucas experienced a rush of power and pride unlike any he'd ever felt and sucked even harder. Ducking lower, he explored Nate's balls, boldly licking them as he continued stroking Nate's cock with quick, firm movements. Remembering a porno he'd watched a dozen or possibly a hundred times, he sucked one of Nate's balls totally into his mouth.

Nate exhaled sharply and shuddered as he came, spurting up onto his chest. Lucas raised his head to watch, and he drank in the sight of Nate with his head thrown back, his smooth chest and hard stomach splattered with semen.

Going up on his hands and knees, Lucas dipped his head and impulsively licked Nate's stomach, savoring the salty taste. Nate chuckled softly and pulled Lucas up for a kiss as he reached down and rubbed Lucas through his jeans.

"You're wearing too many clothes."

There was a knock on the door, and they froze, eyes wide. After a beat, Lucas scrambled off Nate and dived onto the other bed and under the covers as Nate pulled up his duvet. Nate cleared his throat. "Yeah?"

"I'm going out shopping tomorrow with Aunt Linda, so I've left you and Lucas some money on the counter. Have fun in the city. Be home in time to light the menorah, please."

"Okay, Mom."

They listened to her footsteps recede down the hall, both breathing heavily. Then they looked at each other and burst out laughing.

"You need a hand over there?" Nate whispered.

"That would be nice."

Nate flicked off the light and crept over, and they giggled quietly as he jerked Lucas off, which didn't take long at all.

Chapter Five

"THERE YOU GO. Statue of Liberty approaches to starboard, or possibly port. I can never keep them straight."

Lucas nodded. "That's her all right. Looks pretty much like she does on TV."

"You mean you're not filled with a burst of American patriotism at the sight of Lady Liberty?"

"Oh, wait… There it is." Lucas thrust his arms in the air. "USA! USA!"

Laughing, they ignored the stares of people nearby and found an empty bench. The wind was icy out on the water, and most passengers sat inside. Lucas pulled his scarf closer around his throat and wished he'd remembered his hat.

"Wait, stand by the railing," Nate directed Lucas as he pulled a large camera from his messenger bag.

Lucas did as he was told and posed. It felt good to be the focus of Nate's attention, and despite the cold air, a warm glow filled him. He asked, "Your glasses don't bug you when you shoot?"

"Nah. I'm used to it. My eyes hate contacts, and I'm too blind to go without anything. Some people adjust the diopter to compensate for bad vision, but my Nikon has a high eye-point and it works great with my glasses." He huffed out a nervous laugh. "I know I'd probably look better without them, but…"

"What? No way." Lucas glanced around to find they were still alone. "Your glasses are super hot." Nate had seemed so confident about sex that Lucas was surprised to hear any insecurity from him. It was strangely reassuring.

"Yeah?" Nate smiled, clearly pleased.

"Hell yeah."

When Lucas rejoined Nate on the bench after a few more pictures, he leaned back and watched the city skyline get closer. The sun peeked out through the clouds, and Lucas couldn't remember the last time he'd felt so content.

The only thing that could make the moment better would be holding Nate's hand, but he was too afraid to try.

"What's your major?" Nate was watching him with the intent gaze that seemed to be his default expression.

"Chemistry. Premed."

"You want to be a doctor?"

The $64,000 question, as his dad used to say, although Lucas was never sure why. Something about a game show. "Well, I'm really good at science."

"Not exactly a resounding 'yes.'"

"My dad always wanted me to go to med school. I don't want to disappoint him."

Nate was quiet for a moment. "Mom said he died a few months ago. I'm sorry."

"Yeah. Thanks." Lucas tugged off one of his gloves, suddenly preoccupied with an itch on his palm. "You're prelaw, right?"

"Yep." Nate didn't sound thrilled about it.

"Following in your father's footsteps. Well, it's not like Sam's going to."

Nate barked out a laugh that sounded too loud coming from him. "The golden child? Not likely. He'll be too busy basking in the warm memories of his b-ball glory days and probably making a fortune as a salesman at my uncle's company."

"It occurs to me that I don't even know what his major is."

"Technically it's business, but mainly hoops and chicks."

"Okay, I don't understand why he's so special. I mean, he's not a bad guy, but Sam's just such a…"

"Stereotypical jock asshole?"

Laughing, Lucas nodded. "That about sums it up. You're smart and studying to be a lawyer. And you're such an amazing photographer."

Nate shifted on the bench, a little smile tugging at his lips. He took off his glasses and ran his finger over a scratch on the top right of the frame that Lucas assumed was from his camera. "You think so?"

"Of course. Your folks should be putting you on the front cover of their yearly newsletter. They seem like the type to do one."

Gaze still on his glasses in his hands, Nate said, "My parents think Sam walks on water. The thing is, he's always been this…miracle. Mom had a bunch of miscarriages, and they never thought they'd have a baby. When they had Sam, it was the best thing that ever happened to them. Then he turned out to be this amazing athlete, unlike anyone else in my family, and he's been the star of the show ever since."

"But you—"

"Have never been anything to write home about. It's not like my parents don't love me. Sam just became the center of their universe when he was born, and that didn't change when I came along. And if they knew I was queer…" He grimaced and slipped his glasses back on.

"Have you tried talking to them about it? I was terrified of what my dad would say, but he was awesome. Maybe if—"

"No. Everything is fine the way it is. I don't need to tell them."

He wanted to argue, but if Nate wasn't ready to come out, that was his choice. It wasn't as though Lucas had been brave and honest himself at school. "I'm sorry." He couldn't think of anything else to say.

"Don't be." Nate stood and slung his bag over his chest. "Come on, we're almost there."

Lucas knew the conversation was over, and he didn't push it. He felt the urge to grasp Nate's hand again, but instead simply followed him into the surge of passengers downstairs.

An hour later, they stood at the top of the Empire State Building in crisp sunlight, and Lucas marveled at the view of the city. Central Park was an enormous green rectangle holding the surrounding skyscrapers and buildings at bay.

With his camera, Nate seemed to have tunnel vision as he snapped shots of the city below. Lucas divided his time between watching him and peering out at the view, and eventually Nate garnered the majority of his attention.

Nate noticed Lucas's stare after taking about twenty shots of the Flatiron Building. "What?" Lucas swore he saw a blush tint Nate's cheeks.

"You look so happy."

"Yeah. I love photography. I wish…" He shook his head and nodded over his shoulder. "We should check out the other side."

Lucas reached for Nate's arm. "You wish what?"

Nate looked out over the city. After a moment's hesitation, he said, "I wish I could do this all the time."

"Why can't you?"

"Oh, sure. Drop out of prelaw and transfer to Tisch for photography? The 'rents would love that."

"Tisch. Is that in New York?"

"Yeah, it's part of NYU."

Suddenly it made sense to Lucas why Nate hadn't gone away to college. "That's exactly what you want to do isn't it? That's why you went to NYU in the first place."

Nate looked at him sharply and yanked his arm away. "You don't know anything about it."

"You're in third year, right? What are you waiting for?"

"Look, I just can't." Nate jammed the cap back on his camera and zipped it into its case. "It's freezing up here. Let's get some lunch."

"Nate, I don't understand—"

"What was that you were saying about medicine? I think your exact words were that your *father* wanted you to be a doctor."

"That's different." Was it though? Crossing his arms, Lucas shivered. "You're right, let's go inside. It's too cold."

They descended in the elevator, Nate's glasses fogging in the sudden heat, the chatter of a group of German tourists filling the silence. The black cloud hanging over them didn't dissipate as they headed up West Thirty-Fourth Street. Lucas wanted to say the right thing, but with every minute that ticked by, it became more and more awkward.

Despite what they'd shared, it hit home that he and Nate didn't really know each other. Lucas had been feeling so comfortable with him, and now there was only weird, strained silence he didn't have the right words to break.

Nate had told him he wasn't looking for a boyfriend, and perhaps all he wanted was sex and not even friendship. Which was totally fine! Or should have been, but it left Lucas feeling hollow.

Instead of suffering through an awkward lunch, Lucas faked a headache. They spoke to each other in clipped sentences when necessary, and Nate felt like a stranger on the ferry back to Staten Island.

Lucas impulsively accepted an invitation from Sam for pizza and poker with him and his friends that night, even though Sam had clearly only asked because Mrs. Kramer made him. Hopefully poker would involve less small talk than hanging with Mr. and Mrs. Kramer.

Before Lucas and Sam left, they dutifully participated in lighting the menorah. It was the fourth night, and after lighting the middle candle, Mrs. Kramer lit the four candles to the right. Nate disappeared as soon as they were done, and Lucas tried to brush it aside. Much to his surprise, he actually had a good time with Sam's friends, and almost forgot about the tension with Nate.

Almost.

He and Sam came home late, smelling of

pot and the can of beer that had been shaken and sprayed on everyone in attendance in celebration after a guy named Mutt won a particularly big prize. They were only playing with dollar bills, but apparently twenty bucks was a lot to Mutt.

Lucas pushed open the door to Nate's darkened room as quietly as he could, tiptoeing inside. Nate slept, curled toward the windows. After weighing his options—go to bed reeking or risk waking Nate by having a shower—Lucas crept into the bathroom and closed the door behind him. Stripping his clothes off, he stepped into the tub, enjoying the hot water flowing down.

He was on his second shampoo when he realized he wasn't alone. Through the transparent curtain, he saw Nate closing the bathroom door behind him. Leaning against it, Nate watched him.

"Sorry. Did I wake you?" Lucas shifted uneasily. He felt like he was on display in the bright light of the bathroom and resisted the urge to cover himself.

Nate took off his glasses, then his boxers. He slid back the shower curtain. The shampoo trickled down Lucas's forehead, and Nate washed it away with his palm. Stepping back, Lucas silently invited him into the shower.

Since it was far easier than talking, they silently moved into each other's arms and kissed, tongues winding together as their hands explored. Lucas wasn't sure when Nate had picked up the soap, but he leaned into his touch as Nate lathered him.

His cock was at full attention, and Lucas could feel Nate's hardness against his ass as Nate turned him around to face away from the spray of water. His hands still roamed over Lucas, and then one of his fingers pushed just inside Lucas's hole. Lucas tensed, his eyes popping open.

"Relax." Nate whispered in his ear before sucking the lobe gently.

Lucas tried to do as he was told, and Nate's finger probed a little deeper, stretching him. Filling him with a low burn, the pressure of his finger feeling… God, it felt good. *Really* good. He must have said it aloud, because Nate chuckled. "Just wait. It gets better."

"What are you going to do?" Lucas's heart hammered wildly. He knew he was entering uncharted territory.

"I'm going to eat your ass."

The words sounded so wonderfully dirty on Nate's tongue. Lucas had read about rimming, but reading and experiencing were two very different things. He took a deep shuddering breath, excitement thrumming through his veins. He could only say, "Uh…"

Nate smoothed his hands down Lucas's flanks to his hips. "As long as you want me to?"

"Yes, yes. Uh-huh."

Chuckling, Nate kneeled behind him, spreading open his cheeks. At the first touch of Nate's tongue against his hole, Lucas thought he might come right then and there. He leaned forward, bracing his hands wide on the slick tiles as Nate licked and nibbled at his ass, thrusting his tongue inside. If Nate hadn't held him up by his hips, Lucas was sure his legs would collapse as flashes of pleasure shot through his whole body, all the way to the tips of his fingers.

He moaned, breathing heavily as Nate worked magic with his mouth and tongue. When Nate's hand snuck around to stroke Lucas's cock, sparks ignited and his balls tightened. Nate was fucking him with his tongue now, stroking Lucas in time, and Lucas had to press his lips together to keep from shouting.

He shook with his orgasm, whimpering in little gasps as the pleasure overtook him, centered on his cock and his hole, where Nate had his head buried. Propped up by the wall, Lucas tried to catch his breath. Nate's tongue traveled all the way up his spine until Nate nuzzled at the back of his neck.

"Like that?" Nate whispered, nipping at Lucas's skin.

Lucas could only nod. Nate's erection was hot against his ass, and he thought about what it would be like to bend over and let Nate fuck him, to have that hot cock pressing inside. Before he could do anything, Nate turned him around and put Lucas's hand on his rigid cock, urging Lucas to stroke him. He did, and Nate leaned into his touch, his eyes drifting shut.

Nate didn't take long to come, and when he was done, they cleaned up under the hot spray of water. Lucas was just finishing rinsing the leftover shampoo out of his hair when Nate said, "Sorry about today. I was a jerk. I can get like that sometimes."

"It's okay. I didn't mean to push or whatever. I was a jerk too."

Nate turned off the water and stepped out onto the bathmat, wrapping a towel around his lean hips before putting on his steamy glasses. "It wasn't your fault. It's just..." He stopped, his hand on the doorknob.

"What?"

"No one's ever read me that easily before."
Then he was gone, leaving Lucas alone in the
steam.

Chapter Six

WHEN THE PHONE rang in the kitchen, Nate snapped it up off the cradle. "Hello?" He was silent for a moment. "Mom, you know we've got tickets for *Wicked*. In fact, it was you who bought them and insisted I take Lucas to this stupid musical in the first place."

Lucas shifted uncomfortably in his chair at the kitchen table. He hated witnessing fights, even if they were one-sided. They'd been waiting for over half an hour for Mrs. Kramer to return home, since she'd requested they light the menorah with her before going into the city.

"Okay, Mom. I know." After a beat he added, "I love you too." He hung up and turned to Lucas. "Come on, we've got to light this thing and hit the road."

Lucas followed as Nate went to the living

room, pausing to stick his head down the hall toward the den. "Dad! Mom says we should just light it without her tonight."

"Oh." There was a pause, and then Mr. Kramer called, "You boys go ahead without me. And take my car into the city if you want."

Nate's eyebrows raised. "Yeah? Okay, Dad." At the front window, he whispered to Lucas. "He usually doesn't let us within a hundred yards of his Audi."

He struck a match, and Lucas blinked in surprise. "Don't you have to say those things first? The blessings?"

Nate sighed, smiling. "You're worse than my mom." He closed his eyes and spoke the two blessings quickly, and Lucas told himself he shouldn't find it hot. He failed miserably. Nate opened his eyes. "Okay, now you can light the candles."

"Me? I'm really not qualified."

Laughing, Nate struck another match, lighting the middle candle. "This is the *shamash*, which means guard or servant. So we take this"—Nate picked up Lucas's hand and put it on the candle, his palm warm as he covered Lucas's hand with his own—"and then light the other candles with it."

Lucas let Nate's hand guide his as they lit

five other candles, three still unlit. Standing so close to Nate, Lucas felt the warmth of his body and yearned to touch him. They placed the shamash back in its place, but still held it as their eyes met. In the soft, flickering light, Nate had never looked so gorgeous, and Lucas leaned in to kiss him.

"You should get going. Traffic's always bad getting to the theatre district." Mr. Kramer's voice boomed out from the hallway, and Lucas and Nate sprang apart.

Mr. Kramer rounded the corner. "Ah, candles lit. Very good." He pulled out his wallet. "Here's some money for gas, and to have a bite after the show if you want." He handed Nate a wad of bills. "It's very nice of you to entertain Sam's friend." He turned to Lucas before going back to the den. "Merry Christmas."

Lucas blinked, realizing he'd forgotten it was Christmas Eve. "Oh, right. Um, thanks." His first Christmas without his dad was upon him, and he hadn't even noticed it. Guilt soured his stomach, and he had to swallow hard to get rid of the lump in his throat.

In the car, they were quiet as Nate headed to the Verrazano Bridge. "Are you okay? I know it must be hard, with your dad gone and everything. Mom said you don't have any other family?"

"No, not really. And yeah. Thanks." Lucas blew out a long breath. "It sucks. You'd think…" He shook his head.

"What?" Nate reached over and rubbed Lucas's thigh with his palm.

"I knew for months that he was going to die. So did he. He fought hard, but he knew it. So you'd think I'd be more used to it by now or something. Sometimes I'll see something and think, Oh, I need to tell Dad about that. Or, Dad will like that movie. Or whatever. Like I actually forget."

"I think that's normal." Nate rubbed gently, his hand warm on Lucas's thigh. "It's hard too with the holidays. Those old traditions."

The way Nate was touching him—not in a sexy way, just comfort—filled Lucas with longing. He knew he shouldn't get too attached. Nate had made it clear this was only a holiday fling. But maybe…

Forcing a laugh, Lucas said, "Football and junk food isn't really a hallowed family tradition that should be passed on. I don't even like football."

"Well, my dad and Sam will be more than happy to keep the tradition alive tomorrow, I have no doubt."

Lucas laughed. "No doubt." Watching the passing lights of the city as they entered Manhattan, he was quiet for a minute, relishing Nate's caress. Then he said, "Thank you for letting me light the candles. It was…nice." He cringed inwardly at how lame he sounded.

"Yeah." Nate put his hand back on the wheel. "No big deal."

Exactly. No big deal. So don't make one of it, moron, Lucas scolded himself.

When the play let out a few hours later, Lucas and Nate walked into the crisp, clear night, squeezing past the horde of teenage girls waiting at the stage door for the boy bander who was currently playing Boq. Cabs honked incessantly, and the city was alive with light and sound as Nate led him to Rockefeller Center to see the Christmas tree.

Light snow started to fall almost on cue as they approached and shimmied their way into the crowd jostling for a look. Lucas took in the massive tree, which dwarfed the skating rink below, where at least a hundred people circled. A vendor sold hot chestnuts nearby, the smell wafting on the December air. It was like being in a movie.

After a minute, he realized Nate was chuckling. Lucas asked, "What's so funny?"

"You look like Dorothy arriving in Oz."

"Don't make me start singing." Lucas put on a mock serious expression.

"Start? You've been humming and skipping since we left the theater!"

Lucas shoved Nate's arm playfully. "So I like musicals, okay? Besides, don't tell me you didn't enjoy it. You know you got *verklempt* at the end."

"Ohhhh, busting out the Yiddish! Impressive. Very impressive."

"Your bubbe taught me a thing or two the other night."

Nate's cell rang, and while he pushed his way out of the crowd, Lucas followed, gazing around in wonder. Manhattan at night was as vibrant and intoxicating as he always imagined. He thought fleetingly of the sleepy little college town to which he'd soon be returning, where he had felt so alone, and lost a bit of the spring in his step. New York City just seemed so full of *possibility*.

Pocketing his phone, Nate turned to Lucas and eyed him critically, unzipping Lucas's navy jacket. "You've gotta lose the plaid."

"What?" Lucas glanced down at his outfit of jeans, black tee, and plaid shirt over top. "You said this was fine."

"I believe my exact words were that you'd

fit in with the other tourists," Nate teased.

"Okay, so where are we going now?"

"To a flannel-free zone." Nate grinned slyly. "Don't worry, you'll like it."

LUCAS SHIVERED, RUBBING his arms as he tried to restore circulation. The line for the club was long, but Nate had insisted Lucas take off his shirt and jacket and hold them, even though the night was only growing colder. Nate had peeled off his sweater and jacket and was clearly trying not to shiver in his white tank-top style undershirt.

The neon sign on the building screamed *Gomorrah* in scarlet. Lucas was amazed how many people were clubbing on Christmas Eve. He'd really rather just go home and curl up with Nate in one of the twin beds, but he didn't want to be a killjoy.

Sure, the club would be crowded, and the music was so loud the sidewalk practically vibrated with the bass, but when in Rome and all that. Besides, he was with Nate, and it was about time Lucas went to a gay club. He'd seen them in movies and on TV, and his heart skipped excitedly at the thought of actually going into one. It was all very Officially Gay.

Leaning in close, Lucas whispered to Nate, "Have I mentioned I'm not twenty-one?"

"Shhh. Just look cute, which will be easy. I'll handle the rest."

Their turn came at the front of the line, and Nate handed two pieces of ID to the bouncer, who looked them over carefully before giving them back and miraculously waving them inside. In line for coat check, Lucas tried to play it cool, but couldn't.

"What did you give him?"

The thumping bass was muted in the vestibule, but still loud. Glasses fogged, Nate put his lips right up to Lucas's ear, sending a shiver down Lucas's spine. "My driver's license and my library card, plus fifty bucks from my dad."

Lucas didn't stop laughing until they pushed open the doors to the interior of the club. He gazed around, speechless. The cavernous, multilevel circular space was full of men. Young, hot men. Strobe lights pulsed in time to the deafening beat, and Lucas could barely hear himself think.

A few women were here and there, but by and large it was the most male place Lucas had ever been. The most *gay*. It was like heaven. Granted, a very loud, crowded, and sexed-up heaven. But thrilling nonetheless.

Nate must have spotted his friends, because the next thing Lucas knew, Nate took his hand and was pulling him along as they weaved through the crowd surrounding the dance floor. Lucas didn't mind; as long as Nate was holding his hand, he'd go anywhere.

"Hey!" A very good-looking guy with light brown skin and the clearest eyes Lucas had ever seen waved to them. Those eyes raked over Lucas, taking him in from head to toe. He winked at Nate before dropping a quick kiss on his lips. He then turned to Lucas, extending his hand and speaking loudly over the din. "I'm Yaman."

Four cute young men sidled up, all also kissing Nate on the mouth in greeting, which had Lucas staring and trying to hide his surprise. Also the bolt of raging jealousy. Nate had dropped his hand when they'd found their little space in the crowd, and Lucas fought the urge to sling his arm over Nate's shoulders possessively.

After Lucas was introduced to Jamie, Ryan, Gord, and Dave, he tried to pay attention as they all chattered about people he didn't know. It was strange to see Nate with his friends, talking and laughing and being so much more outgoing and confident than he was with his family. Lucas had glimpsed this side of him when they were alone, but it was startling to see him so relaxed.

He tried valiantly not to obsess about whether Nate had slept with any of his friends. He knew it was none of his business, but his mind kept returning to thoughts of Nate with other men. He wanted him all to himself.

When Gord—Lucas was pretty sure it was Gord and not Dave—slung an arm around Lucas's shoulders and asked, "And what's this cutie's story?" Lucas eloquently replied, "Uh…"

Nate swooped in and removed Gord's arm. "Hands off."

Nate's friends all shared a glance with eyebrows raised and chorused, "Ohhh!"

Yaman grinned at Lucas. "You must be something special all right."

Jamie added, "Don't tell me Mr. No Boyfriend—No Way, No How is smitten?"

"Shut up!" Nate jammed his hands in his pockets. "He's just new. I don't want you to scare him off. I don't care what Lucas does."

The hurt struck more deeply than it had any right to. Lucas knew he should laugh it off, but he could only stare at his feet, wishing he was anywhere else. A hand patted his shoulder, and he raised his head to find Ryan smiling kindly. "Don't listen to him. Come on, let's dance."

Lucas shook his head. "I'm a terrible dancer."

"So am I! Come on, baby. We'll be terrible together." Ryan extended his hand, and well, why not? It was better than hanging with Nate, who apparently couldn't care less.

After a couple songs of a jerky approximation of dancing, Lucas relaxed into the music, for once not minding how deafening it was. It make it almost impossible to think, and that was just what he needed.

Yaman and Dave joined them too, and Lucas forced himself not to look for Nate. If Nate didn't care, why should Lucas?

Maybe I shouldn't, but I do anyway.

He told the voice to shut the hell up and jumped around getting sweaty when the new Lady Gaga came on. After a few more songs, he waved to the guys and squeezed off the dance floor, in desperate need of—

There was Nate, holding out a bottle of water. Lucas took it gratefully and chugged half before wiping his mouth. "Um, thanks!" he shouted.

"Do you want a real drink?" Nate yelled back. "I'm driving, but I can buy you one."

"Nah. But thanks." Lucas tried to think of something else to say and failed miserably.

Then Nate blurted, "I'm sorry. I was an asshole. It's not up to me to say who can touch you, and..." He shrugged up his shoulders with a deep breath and let them drop, his words rushing out, barely audible above the blaring techno. "I do care. I care about you. And it's freaking me out."

"I care about you too."

"I just don't know if..." Nate shook his head. "But I was a total asshole, and you don't deserve that."

"I forgive you."

His eyebrows shot up. "Just like that?"

Lucas shrugged. "Yeah. I don't want to be mad at you." He reached out his hand, and Nate took it, drawing him near for a long, slow kiss.

When they parted, Nate asked, "Do you want to dance again?"

"Nah. I just want to watch."

With a nod, Nate led Lucas upstairs to the second floor. A glass-fronted balcony with a railing ran all the way around, and they looked out over the dance floor. Nate stood behind Lucas, his arms snug around Lucas's stomach. It was incredible to be in a place where they were allowed to touch. Where no one would judge or hate them or want to beat them up. The thrill was a heady rush that went right to Lucas's head like champagne.

A mass of male bodies writhed as one below them, bare skin glistening with sweat and glitter that rained down at regular intervals. Some men simply danced, but others rubbed against each other, limbs tangled, kissing desperately. Lucas realized he was half hard, and he wiped sweat from his brow. "It's hot in here," he shouted.

"How's that song go? I think you're supposed to take your clothes off now." Nate nipped Lucas's earlobe.

Gripped by an insane impulse, Lucas peeled off his T-shirt, hooking it through one of his belt loops. Glancing over his shoulder, he saw Nate's expression suddenly grow serious, his eyes dark with desire as he descended on Lucas's mouth, kissing him thoroughly.

Catching his breath, Lucas turned back to the dance floor as Nate moved in even closer, his hands drifting upward, caressing Lucas's chest. Nate raked his short nails through the sprinkling of chest hair before teasing Lucas's nipples, one and then the other. As he sucked at the juncture of Lucas's neck and shoulder, adrenaline sang in Lucas's veins.

When Nate's hand deftly unzipped Lucas's jeans and slipped inside, Lucas glanced around furtively. Bold eyes were on them from all sides, and he found to his shock that being watched sent a bolt of excitement straight to his cock.

As Nate stroked him, he whispered in his ear, "You like that? Like being the center of attention?"

Lucas nodded, licking his lips. He watched the dancers below, arms and legs and torsos slithering through a sea of smoke and glitter. He was a *real* gay man. He'd always felt like an imposter somehow, but now look at him. He was at a gay club being wilder than he'd ever imagined. He didn't need a drink to feel intoxicated.

Nate tightened his fist around Lucas's cock. Then his free hand squeezed down the back of Lucas's briefs, finger touching his hole. Lucas shivered and gasped, his eyes closing. Nate stroked him faster, the tip of his finger dancing around Lucas's pucker.

With the deafening music, Lucas didn't try to bite back his moans of pleasure, and as Nate pushed his finger inside him and crooked it just so, Lucas came with a cry that sounded like it echoed on every side of the club.

Nate supported him, wrapping his arms around Lucas as he kissed his cheek. "I knew you'd be a screamer if you got the chance."

Clinging to the railing, Lucas blinked down at where his semen splattered the glass. He could still feel the heat of anonymous gazes on him, and knew he was blushing furiously. "Holy shit. I can't believe I just did that."

He should have been horrified, but it was exciting to be so *free.* To be surrounded by hundreds of people like him, where he could kiss Nate and not be afraid. More than kiss! He repeated, "Holy shit."

Glasses bumping Lucas's head, Nate kissed his neck as he tucked Lucas back in and zipped him up. "Maybe this'll be a new Christmas tradition?" he shouted as a new song that sounded just like the last one came on, and everyone cheered.

Lucas laughed. "I don't think so." He glanced around, the high of his orgasm wearing off. Fortunately the spectators had moved on. "I wouldn't want to come here too often. Sorry, I'm super lame."

Nate turned him around and brushed back Lucas's sweaty hair. He leaned in close, looping his arms around Lucas's waist. "You want to know a secret? I'm not a huge clubber either. My friends love it, so I end up going with them sometimes. I figured you should have the experience and judge for yourself. It's all right, but I'd really rather be home playing the new *Dead of Winter* expansion pack."

Lucas brightened. "The zombie game? I've always wanted to try it, but my dad couldn't concentrate enough, and I haven't had any friends, so…"

"So what do you say we blow this joint and head home?" He waggled his eyebrows. "Where we can blow each other too."

"I'd say merry Christmas to me."

With a grin, Nate took his hand and led the way, Lucas practically floating behind.

Chapter Seven

LATE THE NEXT afternoon after countless hours spent trying to survive the zombie apocalypse—punctuated by blow jobs and make-out sessions—Lucas and Nate squeezed into the back of the Kramer SUV for a trip to visit Mrs. Kramer's sister. Lucas sat in the middle, and Sam took up so much room to his right that Lucas had no choice but to lean against Nate, their knees pressing particularly firmly.

Nate's cousin Rachel opened the door at the ranch-style house, greeting them— especially Lucas—enthusiastically. The house was smaller than the Kramers', but just as stylishly decorated. Most of the family from the first night of Hanukkah was there, and after lighting the shamash and the menorah's six candles just before sunset, the children began a game of *dreidel* on the carpet.

Lucas sat on the couch, watching the kids spin the four-sided top, making bets with chocolate coins wrapped in gold. Depending on how the dreidel fell, the players sometimes gained more coins or added another to the pot, and on some spins nothing happened at all.

Nate's grandfather joined Lucas and began clapping his hands, singing in a low baritone. "Oh dreidel, dreidel, dreidel, I made you out of clay. Oh dreidel, dreidel, dreidel, with dreidel I shall play."

The children joined in, and Lucas noted with amusement that Nate, watching the game by the window, sang along too. Nate caught his stare and abruptly stopped singing, his flush visible across the room.

When the game was over, Linda, a shorter, plumper version of her sister, and Mrs. Kramer produced a pile of gifts from the other room. The kids squealed in delight as they tore the paper off video games and what Lucas could only guess were the latest trends in Barbie doll fashion. Nate perched on the arm of the couch beside Lucas to unwrap his gift, and Lucas resisted the urge to lean in close.

"So you get presents on Hanukkah? It has nothing to do with it being Christmas today?"

"No presents traditionally, but I guess the

little Jewish kiddies feel left out from the Christmas consumer madness. Adults don't usually get anything. Since most everyone has Christmas Day off work, it's convenient for the family to get together again today."

Nate carefully peeled the paper off a box his parents had given him, revealing a state of the art camera flash that made his eyes widen and a smile split his face.

"Maybe your parents are cooler about the whole photography thing than you think," Lucas whispered.

Nate snorted. "I wouldn't go that far. It's still just my 'little hobby' to them." He got up and hugged his mother and father as Sam let out a surprised gasp.

"Whoa. This is awesome!" He turned around a framed eight by ten black-and-white photograph of himself leaping up to make a basket. Sam grinned and yanked Nate into a bear hug. "Thanks, man. Sorry, I didn't get you anything."

"It's nothing; don't worry. I just thought you'd like it." Nate extracted himself from Sam's embrace as everyone admired the photo. It really was beautiful, capturing Sam in perfect flight.

At dinner—Chinese takeout, which Lucas was told was tradition now—Linda took advantage of the silence while everyone was chewing, telling Nate, "I saw Stephanie Stein's mother last week at synagogue, and she told me Stephanie's back on the market. Such a lovely girl!"

Beside Lucas, Nate stared down at his plate, pushing his chow mein around with his fork, and Lucas could feel the tension coming off him in waves. "I'm sure she's great, but I'm too busy with school right now. Thanks anyway."

"Too busy!" Linda clucked her tongue. "Your brother's never been too busy for girls. She's so pretty! Just take her out to dinner. You'll like her, you'll see," Linda added.

Lucas glanced at Mr. and Mrs. Kramer, who were looking at each other and seemed to be having a telepathic conversation.

Before Nate could reply, Sam spoke up. "Why don't you guys just leave him alone? He likes doing his own thing."

That put an immediate end to the discussion, and after a few moments of awkward silence, Mr. Kramer complimented Linda enthusiastically on the sweet and sour chicken balls, everyone echoing his sentiments.

Under the table, Lucas covered Nate's sock-clad foot with his own. Nate shot him a smile and speared his last chicken ball, putting it onto Lucas's plate. Lucas smiled back, and as he ate it, he realized Mr. and Mrs. Kramer were watching them, their expressions seemingly neutral.

Still, Lucas's face went hot, and he moved his foot away, dropping his gaze to his plate, suddenly very interested in his Peking duck.

As soon as they were inside Nate's room again, Nate shoved Lucas up against the door and kissed him hard. He pushed Lucas's legs apart with his knee and rubbed their crotches together as his tongue plundered Lucas's mouth.

Lucas gasped for a breath, a grin tugging on his lips. "Does 'The Dreidel Song' always make you this horny, Nathaniel?"

Nate practically growled, spinning Lucas around and steering him toward the far bed before taking his desk chair and jamming it under the door handle. Lucas waited, growing more and more excited by the lust in Nate's eyes.

Nate rustled around in one of the desk drawers, not bothering to turn on a light. The curtains were open, and the streetlight cast pale white light and long shadows across the room. When Nate peeled his clothes off, Lucas followed suit, and soon they were both naked and kissing on the tiny bed.

Nate pressed something into his hand, and Lucas realized he was holding a condom. His eyes jerked up to meet Nate's. "You want…"

Nate's gaze was steady and direct. "I want you to fuck me."

Lucas gulped. *Merry Christmas indeed.*

After putting his glasses on the side table, Nate kneeled and popped the lid off a tube of lubricant. He reached his hand behind himself. Lucas realized he was lubing himself up, and his cock twitched in anticipation. They were really going to do it.

He was going to fuck another man.

Nate fingered himself, his pale chest gleaming in the streetlight. A small smile graced his lips, and Lucas took a deep, calming breath, his pulse racing. He tore open the foil package, rolling the condom down over his cock. With a slick hand, Nate stroked Lucas's shaft, and Lucas tried to keep his cool.

When Nate got on his hands and knees, Lucas almost lost it, but he clambered up behind him, reaching out and holding Nate by the hips. He positioned the head of his cock at Nate's hole, taking another breath.

This was it. He'd seen enough porn to know what he was doing, right?

"*Fuck me,*" Nate gritted out.

Heart thumping, Lucas squeezed inside him, moving into the tight, incredible heat inch by inch. Nate pushed back, squeezing his muscles and establishing a rhythm. Lucas began thrusting in and pulling almost all the way out, pleasure shooting through his cock. After a tentative start, he felt like he got the hang of it, grabbing one of Nate's shoulders for better leverage as he worked his ass.

Nate grunted and breathed heavily, and their skin grew slippery with sweat as Lucas pumped into him. "Harder," Nate demanded.

Lucas pistoned his hips forcefully into Nate's tight heat, panting for air and biting his lip to stop from crying out. He was inside another man. He was inside *Nate*; he was fucking *Nate*. He never wanted it to end. He wanted to stay inside him forever, locked together in abandon and bliss.

Of course, he was about to shoot his load. Shaking, he stopped moving for a moment, willing his body to obey him as he sucked in air. Sweat dampened his brow. When he felt back in control, he rocked his hips forward again, plunging in and out of Nate's ass.

Reaching back, Nate took Lucas's hand

and placed it on his cock as they writhed together. Lucas stroked him rapidly, jerking Nate's cock in tandem with the almost manic thrusting of his hips. Nate squeezed down with his ass, and then he was shaking as he came.

The pressure and heat on his cock was intense, and with a cry, Lucas shot into the condom, closing his eyes as the orgasm rocked his body. He collapsed on top of Nate, both of them breathing hard, skin slick. After a minute, he reluctantly pulled out and stood on quivering legs.

After he disposed of the condom, wrapping it in almost an arm's length of toilet paper just in case Mrs. Kramer was the nosy type, Lucas returned to the bedroom. He hovered at the foot of Nate's bed, not sure what to do. Nate was sprawled on his stomach even though it had to be wet, taking up the whole space.

Lucas suddenly felt very exposed, and he quickly put on his T-shirt and pajama bottoms. Turning to Nate, he sat on the side of his mattress and waited. Nate's eyes were closed, so apparently he was just going to sleep now? Was Lucas being creepy sitting there watching him? He'd just been *inside* Nate's body. Surely that meant something?

Eyes still closed, Nate crooked his finger. "C'mere."

Lucas knelt beside Nate's bed. He cleared his throat. "I guess we should get some sleep."

Opening his eyes, Nate reached his hand behind Lucas's head and pulled him close for a long, slow kiss. "That was amazing." A rush of pride made Lucas smile, and Nate tapped him on the nose affectionately. "You're a natural."

Saying thanks would sound kind of stupid, so Lucas just kissed Nate again before climbing into the other bed. They were only a couple of feet apart, but Lucas yearned to press against Nate's warm body and fall asleep holding him.

Stop it. This doesn't mean anything. It's just sex. A holiday fling. That's all.

Still, as his eyes grew heavy, Lucas couldn't help but *wish*.

THE NEXT DAY dawned bright and sunny, so Mrs. Kramer declared it a perfect time to visit the Bronx Zoo. Lucas hadn't expected the zoo to be so sprawling or state of the art, and the only thing that could have made wandering the exhibits better would have been holding

Nate's hand.

He longed to touch him all the time and considered dragging him into a bathroom stall after lunch for a quick grope. Mr. Kramer put a kibosh on that by coming to the bathroom too. Nate had winked teasingly at Lucas just briefly at the urinals, so apparently Lucas needed to do a better job of hiding his sexual frustration.

After a volunteer gave them a lesson on lemurs near the end of the afternoon, Lucas and the Kramers wandered through the gift shop. Lucas was drawn to the magnets, and as he plucked a gorilla from the metal holder, he said to Nate, "My dad would—"

The next words lodged in his throat, and Lucas realized he hadn't thought of his father once all day. His dad had loved collecting silly magnets everywhere they went, covering their fridge from top to bottom.

Like a finger removed from a dam, guilt and grief flooded him, and he blinked back tears, the magnet clattering to the floor. He was only vaguely aware of Nate's hand on the small of his back, leading him out into the brisk air. He tried to breathe, leaning against the wall of the building.

From the corner of his eye, he saw the Kramers exit the store. Nate drew them away, murmuring, and Lucas willed himself to get a grip. After a few deep breaths, he walked over to them and said, "Sorry. Just had a moment. I'm fine."

Mrs. Kramer clucked her tongue. "Dear, you don't need to put on a brave face. We know how hard it must be for you. If you want to talk about it, we're all here to listen."

"Why?" Lucas blurted. He shook his head. "I'm sorry. I—thank you. What I mean is, I don't know why you're being so nice to me. You don't even know me."

Nate said, "Anyone who has the patience to room with Sam and not murder him—"

"Is always welcome in our home," Mr. Kramer finished, giving Nate a good-natured glare. To Lucas, he added, "It's been a pleasure getting to know you this week. I hope we'll be seeing much more of you in the future."

Lucas felt so stupid for causing a scene, and they were being so nice about it. He smiled weakly. "Thank you again. But Sam will be graduating and…"

Mrs. Kramer smiled. "Well, you and Nathaniel seem to be getting along like gangbusters. Aren't you?"

Lucas said, "Uh…" *Don't blush. Don't blush.* "Yeah."

She looked to Nate, who shrugged and nodded at the same time. There was something about her smile and a strange tension in the air that had Lucas's head whirling.

Does she know?

Before the moment could get any weirder, Mr. Kramer thankfully announced he was getting hungry and it was time to head home. He and Mrs. Kramer kept up a steady stream of chatter in the front seat on the drive, their forced cheer evident.

Lucas stared out the window, more aware than ever that no matter how kind the Kramers were to him, his father—his only real family—was gone. Nate was right beside him but out of reach. He didn't want a relationship; he'd said so, no matter how close Lucas felt to him. After the holidays, Lucas would be on his own again.

The evening passed in a haze—lighting the menorah and then watching another movie, this one about creatures from the deep attacking Earth. Lucas picked at a slice of pizza and told Mrs. Kramer he was fine. When the credits rolled, he excused himself for the night. Nate followed a few minutes later, shutting his bedroom door quietly behind him. Lucas climbed into bed, Nate watching him silently.

"I just want to sleep tonight, okay?" Lucas said. What he actually wanted was to simply be held, but could he ask that of Nate? It was only supposed to be a fling, and as kind as Nate was being, surely cuddling crossed some line.

Nate nodded, and soon he was in his own bed, the lights out. Curling on his side toward the door, Lucas tried to clear his mind, but it was useless. He couldn't stop thinking of the stupid gorilla magnet. His dad's magnet collection was piled in a box in some storage unit in Michigan with the rest of the stuff they'd had in their last apartment. Lucas had barely been able to bring anything to school, and when would he have an actual *home* again?

A sob gripped him, cutting off his breath, and he buried his face in his pillow to stifle the ones that followed. When his father had finally slipped away, Lucas hadn't cried. The nurses had hugged him and told him to let it out, but he'd insisted he was fine. Now the tears wouldn't stop.

After a few moments, the mattress dipped, and Nate's long frame spooned up behind him, his arms snaking out to hold Lucas close. As Lucas wept, Nate caressed his hair, whispering calming words in Hebrew that sounded like a lullaby.

Lucas wasn't sure how long he cried before his breathing became easier. Nate still soothed him, and soon Lucas wanted more. *Needed* more. He shifted, and in a tangle of limbs, Nate rolled on top of him on the narrow bed. Lucas pulled Nate's head down for a kiss, and their tongues wound together as Lucas's hands roamed over Nate, sliding up beneath his T-shirt.

Nate's body on top of his was heady, but not enough. "Please," Lucas breathed.

Nate pulled back and watched him for a moment, squinting in the darkness, asking without saying a word if Lucas was sure. "Please," Lucas repeated. He pulled Nate's shirt over his head, and soon their pajamas were tossed aside.

Nate was up and back before Lucas knew it. He bent Lucas's knees, placing his feet flat on the mattress, kneeling in front of him. Squeezing the lube into his palm, Nate warmed it up before his fingers found Lucas's hole, gently working the slick gel inside. He started with one finger, lightly stroking Lucas's cock with his other hand. Then two fingers.

When he had the condom on and lubed, he moved closer and placed Lucas's legs up onto his shoulders, opening him. Lucas had never felt more vulnerable, but he only shivered with anticipation. He trusted Nate completely.

Nate slowly pushed his way inside, and Lucas felt like he was tearing open. His eyes watering, he gasped as the pain blossomed. Nate leaned down, kissing him tenderly all over his face: cheeks, forehead, and eyes. "Just breathe," he whispered, and Lucas felt a calm come over him, his body relaxing despite the pain.

Bit by bit, Nate moved farther inside him, the stretch both almost unbearable and something he never wanted to stop. They were both breathing heavily, and sweat glistened on Nate's forehead in the streetlight.

When Nate was almost all the way in, he hit a spot that made Lucas see stars, a moan of pleasure slipping from his lips. With another kiss and a little smile, Nate began shallow little thrusts, hitting that spot every time.

Lucas began moving with him, the pain ebbing away to become pure pleasure. Nate pressed Lucas's knees to his chest and drove into him, grasping one of his hands. Lucas felt like he was in a dream, drifting in a world where nothing else existed but him and Nate. Their eyes locked together as their bodies flexed and rocked. Nate was *inside* him, and Lucas could feel it in his soul.

His cock was hard and leaking, squeezed between their bodies as Nate increased his rhythm. He found the spot again, grunting softly as he hit it over and over. Lucas couldn't stifle his cry as he came, his orgasm ripping through him. As he shook, Nate thrust sharply two more times before shuddering in release.

Lucas winced when Nate pulled out of him. Nate dropped a kiss to his shoulder, murmuring something Lucas couldn't make out. Sitting up, Nate tossed the tied-off condom into the garbage pail by his desk. Before Lucas could even ask him to stay, he pulled the covers up over them, wrapping Lucas tightly in his arms.

Nate kissed Lucas's ear and whispered, "Sleep."

The fracturing grief for his father had receded for the moment, and he felt whole in a way he couldn't explain as he closed his eyes in Nate's arms. Lucas hadn't meant to fall in love, but he realized with a sense of wonder that was exactly what he'd done.

Chapter Eight

RUNNING, NATE AND Lucas barely made it on board the ferry before it left the dock, and they laughed, their icy exhalations puffing out in front of them. Most passengers crowded inside, but Lucas liked to watch the city glide by. On the upper deck, he and Nate leaned against the railing and caught their breath.

It had been a perfect day.

The Met was crowded with holiday visitors, but Lucas barely noticed. He and Nate were in their own little world, and Lucas vowed to himself to just enjoy it and worry about the future when it came.

Of course, as he stood shoulder to shoulder with Nate, watching the Statue of Liberty in the distance, his mind wandered to his inevitable return to school. He sighed audibly, and Nate nudged him gently, an eyebrow raised.

"I'm just thinking about the new year. Going back to school." Lucas's dour tone pretty much said it all.

Nate was quiet for a few moments. "So why are you going back?"

"Because I have to." Where else would he go?

"What are you doing at Brookfield? Even Sam notices you're miserable."

"What? You and Sam were talking about me?"

"Not in a bad way, but my usually clueless brother knows you're not happy there." He took a breath, as if steeling himself. "You could move here in the summer. Transfer schools; there are about a million to choose from. Figure out what you really want to do with your life."

The thought of returning to Brookfield and the noisy dorm, going back to his chemistry books and the degree he didn't truly want, filled Lucas with dread. Maybe Nate was right. What was stopping him from coming to New York and living his own life?

His father had wanted him to be happy, and Lucas had pretended for long enough that his father's dreams for him were his own. "Well, it would be pretty awesome to live in

New York if I could afford it. I mean, I have money from my dad, so I guess I could." A thrill zipped through him. "I guess… I guess there really is nothing stopping me. Whoa."

"Blowing your mind, huh?" Nate grinned.

"A little bit. Brookfield was where my dad wanted to go, but he didn't have the grades. So when I got in, he was over the moon." Lucas shivered as frigid wind gusted, his ears stinging. He stupidly had forgotten his hat. "But he'd want me to be happy."

"Of course he would."

Lucas couldn't stop smiling. "What about you? Are you going to quit law? Switch to photography?"

"What? No. I'm not good enough," Nate said dismissively.

"Yes, *you are*."

"You're being nice, but I don't have the talent." He smiled ruefully and muttered under this breath, "*My little hobby.*"

"Your mother has no idea what you're capable of. You do *so* have the talent. You're afraid to take the risk, but you expect *me* to."

Nate was silent for a long moment, peering out to the horizon and the city slipping away. Finally he sighed. "You're right. I'm a hypocrite." He wrapped his arms around himself, shivering as the wind whipped off the water.

"You don't have to be. Neither of us is happy. We need to make a change. We could do it together."

Nate looked at him. "Together?"

"Oh, I mean…not… I don't…" Lucas took a deep breath. Time to stop being afraid. "Screw it. Yes. Together. You and me. I really like you. And I know you don't want that, a boyfriend, so I'm probably wasting my breath, and this is just a holiday fling."

Nate straightened his glasses, and Lucas realized he did it when he was nervous. After a deep breath, Nate said, "I've been thinking about that. You're only a few hours away. Sam goes on the road a lot for basketball in the new year, and he's going to Daytona for spring break. I could visit."

Lucas tried to tamp down his rush of excitement and failed completely. Then a thought hit him, and his smile vanished. "What about when we're not together? Will you still be seeing other guys?"

Nate leaned closer. "I don't want to see anyone but you, Lucas."

Warm happiness exploded in Lucas's chest like the creature in *Alien*. "I thought you weren't looking for a boyfriend."

"I wasn't." Nate smiled crookedly. "I

guess one found me. If you want me."

Not caring if anyone was watching, Lucas threw his arms around him. "I want."

Nate held him close, their cheeks pressed together. Lucas watched the sun sink over the distant skyscraper in a blaze of red and orange. He had a boyfriend. He might move to New York City. He had a *boyfriend.* Maybe holiday miracles really did happen.

When Nate laughed and said, "Maybe," Lucas realized he'd said it aloud. He only hugged Nate tighter.

IN THE UBER, Nate checked his phone. "We missed lighting the menorah on the last night of Hanukkah. If we miss synagogue, I'm dead meat." When they'd gotten home to a darkened house, they'd quickly changed, Lucas borrowing a tie and jacket.

"But I thought you weren't that observant," Lucas said.

"We're not, but we always have to go to synagogue at least once every holiday, or we'll never hear the end from Papa. I kind of like it, actually."

Hopping out in front of the temple, Nate took the empty steps two at a time before he jolted to a halt and pulled a rounded, dark gray suede piece of material from his pocket. He placed it on the back of his head.

Lucas said, "Okay, this is going to sound like a stupid question, but—"

"How does it stay on?" Nate laughed. "Years of experience." He pulled another piece of material out of his pocket, this one black. "You, however, get a bobby pin for your *yarmulke*."

Lucas stood still while Nate gently pinned it in place. Their heads were close together, and Nate's warm breath ghosted over Lucas's cheek. Nate stood back. "There you go. Looks good. What about me?" He laughed suddenly, rolling his eyes. "I know, I look like a complete dork."

Fat snowflakes had begun to fall, nestling in Nate's hair and spotting his glasses, and Lucas told him the truth. "You look beautiful."

Nate leaned closer, their lips inches apart. Just then, a van pulled up, unloading a chattering family who rushed by them up the steps. Lucas and Nate followed, finding a seat near the back.

Lucas gazed in wonder at the blue and gold ceiling soaring high above. A center aisle separated rows of pews, and ornate chandeliers hung in pillared archways along each side of the room, with a gallery of extra seating on the left and right through the arches on the second level. It was a full house.

The rabbi spoke of freedom, and conquering fear and despair. As the service went on, Lucas was filled with a sense of peace he couldn't remember ever experiencing. He thought of his father and smiled. The pain was still there, but Lucas knew he would get through it.

Glancing down to his left, he saw Nate's hand on the bench beside him. Sliding his palm over the polished wood, he touched Nate's pinky finger with his own. He would have been satisfied with just that small contact, but a few moments later, Nate flipped his hand over. As the congregation began singing, Lucas covered Nate's palm with his own, threading their fingers together.

Lucas didn't understand the words, but he tried to sing along anyway.

After the service and socializing, Lucas and the Kramers pushed open the doors of the synagogue to discover the world had been covered in white. Large flakes of snow floated down, blanketing everything and giving the night an unnatural, serene brightness, the wind gentle now. They all paused to admire the beauty of the winter's first real snowfall.

Mrs. Kramer's fingers brushed over Lucas's yarmulke playfully. "It suits you, Lucas. You'll have to come and stay for Passover." She planted a kiss on his cheek. "And I won't take no for an answer!" Hooking her arm through her husband's, she led the way down the snowy steps. "Let's go home and eat."

Nate and Lucas followed side by side, neither of them able to hide their smile.

In the Kramers' living room, the menorah candles had burned out, and Lucas was sorry he hadn't had a chance to see all eight of them burning. Maybe next year…

Mrs. Kramer tutted as she examined her black high-heeled shoes. "I wouldn't have worn these if I'd known it would snow. At least the salt wasn't out yet."

Mr. Kramer took the shoes from her. "I'll give them a good polish. Don't worry." He kissed her cheek, and she beamed at him.

Lucas found himself smiling as he watched. He caught Nate's eye, wishing he could show him affection like that. *My boyfriend. I have a boyfriend!* Nate gave him a little smile. Maybe they could go upstairs quickly and just kiss for a minute or two.

Then Sam said, "What are you two grinning about?"

"Huh?" Lucas jerked his head around. "Nothing. Just... Um, hungry. Looking forward to dinner."

Mrs. Kramer said, "Well, we have a lovely meal waiting. Everyone to the table."

"And where was tonight's delicacy ordered from?" Mr. Kramer asked.

"Baggio's," she answered. "Veal tortellini, our favorite burrata and tomato salad, that mushroom risotto Nathaniel loves, and garlic bread of course. And panna cotta for dessert." To Lucas, she added, "I'm sure you've noticed I'm not much for cooking."

"I'm not either, so."

They all laughed, and Lucas ran a hand through his hair, his yarmulke coming loose. "Oh! Sorry."

Chuckling, Nate came close and reached up to unpin it completely. "It's okay. We only wear them at temple." He straightened Lucas's hair, sending tingles down Lucas's spine. He couldn't wait until they were alone again and—

"So are you guys boning, or what?"

Lucas's heart seized violently, his stomach lurching and threatening to bring up the burger he'd had for lunch. Nate whipped his hands back to his sides, looking like he was choking on his tongue, his face beet red.

The Kramers turned in the wide doorway to the kitchen, mouths open. Mrs. Kramer snapped, "*Samuel!*"

"What?" He rolled his eyes. "Sorry. Are you two *making love?*" As Nate sputtered, Sam added, "Come on, dude. We know you're gay."

Chest rising and falling rapidly, Nate looked between Sam and their parents. He crossed his arms, and Lucas wanted to step closer so Nate knew he wasn't alone, but didn't think it would help. He jammed his hands in his pockets, waiting.

Mr. Kramer sighed. "Son, we've been waiting for you to tell us. Was that the wrong thing to do?"

"Unless we're mistaken after all?" Mrs. Kramer asked.

Nate laughed harshly. "You'd be relieved if you were."

She jerked her head back an inch, blinking. "No. That's not true at all."

"Oh, come on, Mom." Nate's tense jaw worked, his nostrils flaring. "I know you think gay people are *vulgar.*"

"I do not!" She stood up straighter, her husband placing a comforting hand on her shoulder, frowning at Nate.

"Dude, what the hell are you talking

about?" Sam lifted his meaty hands in the air. "Mom and Dad are totally cool with it."

Mr. Kramer said, "Nate, we love you. We haven't wanted to push. Rabbi Lowenstein said to let you come out when you were ready."

"You told the rabbi?" Nate shouted. "Great, now everyone probably knows. What about the rest of the family?"

"No," Mr. Kramer answered. "First off, Rabbi Lowenstein would never betray our trust. We asked for his counsel in confidence. And we haven't told anyone else in the family, although I'm sure some of them suspect. It's absolutely your choice as to when you want to tell them."

"Why did you say that? That I find gay people 'vulgar'?" Mrs. Kramer asked, her lips quivering along with her voice.

When Nate spoke, at least he wasn't shouting. In fact, it was barely more than a whisper. "There was a pride parade on the news. Ten years ago now, I guess. There were guys in Speedos on a float, and you said it was vulgar. With such disdain."

She exhaled sharply. "Well, men thrusting their pelvises while clad only in tiny bathing suits *is* vulgar. I've never been one for such displays. Bathing suits belong on the beach. It has nothing to do with being gay."

Mr. Kramer said, "She's never liked beauty pageants for the same reason. And there isn't even any pelvis thrusting in those."

Tears glistened in her eyes. "Nate, have you thought all this time that I wouldn't approve?"

Adam's apple bobbing, Nate nodded, staring at the beige carpet. His mother crossed the space between them in a heartbeat, wrapping him in her arms. Tears slipped down her cheeks, and he bent to rest his head on her shoulder, hunching since she was shorter.

"You couldn't be more wrong," she said. "I love you. I want you to be happy. That's what we all want."

Lucas's eyes burned, and he blinked rapidly, jumping when Mr. Kramer squeezed his shoulder. "Lucas, I know we've only just met you, but I hope you know you're very welcome here. Gay, straight, whatever. It doesn't matter to us."

"I... Thank you." Lucas swallowed hard, his voice trembling. "I am. Gay, I mean. We..." He glanced at Nate, who raised his head and stepped back from his mom, swiping at his eyes.

Nate nodded. "We really like each other.

We're going to visit each other whenever we can in the new year and see what happens."

"I knew it!" Sam crowed.

Nate muttered, "Shut up," but there was no heat to it. He looked between his parents. "I'm sorry I didn't tell you before. That I'm gay. I really didn't think you'd be okay with it."

Now tears formed in Mr. Kramer's eyes. "I'm sorry we gave you that impression." He pulled Nate into a hug, and Lucas blinked rapidly, warmth spreading through his chest, his breathing steady now.

Sam punched Lucas in the shoulder playfully. "Man, it must be torture for you rooming with me and seeing me naked and stuff. But thanks for not hitting on me or anything."

A giggle bubbled up and Lucas tried to keep a straight face. He failed miserably, and Nate even smiled as he separated from his dad.

Sam shrugged. "What? I'm just saying! Hello, I'm hot."

Lucas nodded, trying to stifle his laughter. "It's a challenge, Sam. I appreciate your understanding."

"Gay people are just like everyone else, and I was thinking it would be hard to live with some hot chick I couldn't bang."

Nate eyed him skeptically. "You're really okay with me being gay? Dating Lucas?"

"Totally, bro."

Nate smiled, shaking his head. "I thought you'd hate me."

Sam was taken aback. "Dude, I could never *hate* you." He reached out and jerked Nate into a hug, slapping his back forcefully. "You're my brother. So what if you fuck guys?" He winced. "Sorry, Mom and Dad. I mean *make love* with guys."

Lucas said, "We really appreciate your support. It means a lot."

"Hey, we're friends, right? Of course I support you." Sam turned to Lucas and hugged him too.

As Sam slapped his back, Lucas grinned. "Definitely friends." He was happy to discover that he really meant it.

"Well. Now that we have that settled." Mrs. Kramer blew her nose delicately, folding the tissue after. "Our dinner's keeping warm in the oven, and we don't want it to dry out. Let's sit around the table instead of in front of the TV."

Nate and Lucas shared a smile as they followed toward the dining room. Lucas reached out and squeezed Nate's hand.

"Oh, one more thing," Mrs. Kramer said,

turning back. "Now, I'm sure you know all about safety. In regards to…" She waved her hand.

Nate groaned. "Dad, make her stop!"

Mr. Kramer slipped his arm around his wife's shoulders. "Come along now, dear. Let's celebrate the last night of Hanukkah and leave the safe sex lecture for another day."

"Don't you mean safe *making love*?" Sam asked as he followed, apparently endlessly amused by his own joke. "Hey, since we're having Italian, we get to drink real wine with dinner, right? Not that sweet crap. I mean *stuff*."

As his family disappeared around the corner, Nate stopped. He appeared slightly dazed, his glasses askew. Lucas reached out to straighten them as Nate asked, "Did that really just happen?"

"It did."

"I can't believe it. Seems like I've been a real idiot."

"Seems like."

Nate burst out laughing. "Hey!" He frowned in mock offense. "I thought boyfriends were supposed to be supportive."

"My bad." With a glance around, Lucas gave Nate a quick kiss. "I'll make it up to you later."

"Deal." Nate grinned. Then he shook his

head. "I can't believe my family is being so cool about this. I guess miracles really do happen at Hanukkah."

Lucas gave him another kiss. "I guess they do."

Epilogue

One Year Later

FROM JUST INSIDE the doorway, Mrs. Kramer surveyed the studio apartment, which now appeared even smaller thanks to the arrival of Nate's belongings. "Well, it's…cozy." She held her fur-trimmed leather gloves, her long black jacket still buttoned.

Lucas shimmied between some boxes and the left-hand wall and made it into the narrow kitchen, which was separated from the living room by an island counter. "Can I get you a bottle of water?" He'd worked up a sweat and had stripped off his plaid shirt, wearing just a white tee and jeans.

"No, dear, we really can't stay," Mrs. Kramer replied. She looked to the immediate right at the so-called bedroom, which was really more of a nook behind a half-wall, barely big enough for the double bed Lucas had brought from Michigan after sorting through the storage unit.

He'd gotten rid of a lot of stuff, but having his dad's brown leather couch and armchair against the right-hand wall in the living room made the bare-walled apartment feel like home already. The TV was still in its box, along with most of Lucas's possessions.

Nate and his father nudged Mrs. Kramer out of the doorway and inside, carrying the last of Nate's boxes. Mr. Kramer stretched his back with a soft groan and said, "All right, you're all set."

Mrs. Kramer scoffed. "Hardly. Look at how much needs to be unpacked. I thought Rabbi Lowenstein said this was a 'spacious' studio? And your view is a brick wall. Good thing you're on the tenth floor so you can glimpse the sky." She tutted.

Nate squeezed between stacks of boxes and grabbed water from the otherwise-empty fridge. "It is, Mom. We've looked at a thousand crappy apartments since the beginning of summer. This one is amazing for the price. Rabbi Lowenstein's cousin's sister's aunt cut us a great deal."

"After six months of sharing Nate's room at the house, I'm sure this will feel like luxury," Mr. Kramer said.

"Totally," Lucas agreed, then hastily added, "Not that your home isn't lovely! I appreciate you letting me stay so much." He'd transferred to NYU after finishing his year at Brookfield, and the Kramers had been incredibly generous by letting him move in with them while he and Nate hunted for an apartment, which was a blood sport in New York City.

The Kramers smiled, and Mr. Kramer clapped Lucas's shoulder. "We know, son. We also know how exciting it is to have a place of your own."

"And Hell's Kitchen has come a long way," Mrs. Kramer said. "So many restaurants right around the corner. Although it's really quite noisy." A siren wailed distantly on cue.

"Come on, Deanna. Boys, we'll see you soon. Hanukkah starts tomorrow, so we'll expect you for dinner. Call if you need anything." Mr. Kramer ushered his wife to the door.

She gave Nate a long hug and kissed him tenderly on the forehead before stepping back. "Be good, *bubala*."

As soon as the door closed behind them after more goodbyes, Lucas met Nate's eyes across the stacks of boxes, and they grinned.

Nate gazed around, taking in the bathroom squeezed right across from the foot of the bed in its nook. "What are we going to do with all this *space?*"

Lucas laughed. "Just wait until you see the east wing. It's impressive."

"But it's *ours.*" Nate took his phone from his pocket and snapped a few shots. "I'll take some real pics when we're unpacked, but I want to document the process."

"Should I model, Mr. Photographer?"

"Always." Nate winked and took a few more pictures as Lucas made faces and posed with boxes.

Nate had applied to Tisch for photography without mentioning it to his parents, figuring he'd see if he got in first. Naturally he did—Lucas had been confident it was a slam dunk—and he'd broken the news to his parents. They hadn't taken it very well at first, but had either come around or resigned themselves. Either way, they were supportive.

Nate eyed the bed beyond the half-wall. "We finally have a real bed that'll fit both of us. I can't wait to sleep with you every night."

While of course they'd still had sex in Nate's room, actual sleep had usually occurred in their twin beds. "Just sleep, hmm?"

"Fucking goes without saying. Duh." He

bit his lip. "Speaking of which, maybe we should christen our new bed. You can scream as loud as you want."

Lucas didn't have to be asked twice. They sidestepped the boxes, falling back on the bare mattress. Nate's weight on top of him felt so good—so right. He carefully took off Nate's glasses and put them on the shelf built into the half-wall separating the bed from the entry and living room. Then he yanked Nate's sweater over his head and kissed his smooth chest, teeth on Nate's pink nipples, making him squirm and moan.

The taste of Nate's salty skin was heady. Lucas rolled over, his mouth moving over Nate's body, peeling away clothing as he continued until Nate was naked beneath him, both of them kicking off their sneakers and peeling away socks.

"I need to fuck you. Or you fuck me. Whatever. I need to feel you." Nate gritted the words out, and his already-hard dick was proof of them.

Lucas sat up on his knees and quickly stripped off his clothes. "Shit. Where did we pack the lube?" They'd stopped using condoms now that they were completely committed to each other and had clean bills of health.

"In the bathroom box? Oh, wait, wait. In my wallet. They were giving out those little packets on campus for some sex-ed drive or something."

Lucas dug through Nate's pockets and came up with the lube, tossing the packet to Nate. "Put it on yourself." Nate opened it and rubbed the lube between his palms before slicking himself as Lucas straddled his hips.

Nate stroked himself with one greased hand and the other found Lucas's hole. He pushed his fingers inside roughly. "Fuck, you're tight. You look so hot. I can't believe we're actually here. In our own place."

"Me either." Heart pounding, desperation ignited in Lucas's veins. Even though they'd given each other hand jobs in the shower that morning, he felt like it had been forever ago. He moved over Nate's dick, maneuvering himself into position.

With a loud moan, he slid down and the head of Nate's cock stretched him painfully. He bit his lip as he forced himself down the shaft.

"Whoa. I don't want to hurt you." Nate held Lucas's hips firmly, stopping his downward movement.

Lucas shuddered, the burn in his ass almost too much as he lowered himself. *Almost.*

"I want to feel you tomorrow. I want your cock. I need it."

Eyes dark with lust, Nate reached for his glasses. "You're so beautiful. I could watch you all day. I want to take your picture like this. With my cock inside you." He bent his legs and thrust his hips up. Lucas cried out as he impaled himself fully, the pleasure and pain combining as he rode Nate. "Oh God, oh God."

"That's it. Be as loud as you want."

Lucas squeezed his ass on Nate's dick as he bucked up and down. His own cock was hard as rock, and Nate reached out for it, stroking roughly. Lucas cried out over and over. "Oh, oh, God."

Sweat dampened his brow and the back of his neck, their skin slick where their bodies met. A sense of abandon came over Lucas, a complete lack of inhibition as he slammed down on Nate's cock over and over again, making two bodies one.

"I love your ass. You're so tight, oh God," Nate muttered, and he squeezed Lucas's dick, his thumb flicking over the head. "Love coming inside you. Want you to come all over me."

Suddenly Lucas came in a rush, spraying Nate as he clamped down on Nate's cock.

Lucas's cries would probably wake the dead, but he let them rip. Nate fucked up into him almost frantically, head tilted back and eyes closed. Voice hoarse, Lucas urged him on. "Fill me up."

After another few thrusts, Nate shuddered, his semen spilling deep in Lucas's ass. Lucas squeezed, trying to milk out every drop before flopping down on Nate's chest, kissing his throat. They panted, bodies a wet and sticky mess, and Nate lightly ran his fingers up Lucas's spine.

Lucas murmured, "I guess we should unpack."

"Five more minutes. Or ten."

After they cleaned up, Lucas yawned on the mattress, still naked. It had been a hella long drive from Michigan the day before. Maybe he could just close his eyes for a few minutes…

He wasn't sure what time it was when he woke with a fluffy duvet tucked around him. Stretching, he reluctantly sat up. The overhead light was on in the kitchen, illuminating the whole apartment, and Lucas was surprised to see through the windows it was already dark outside.

Peering over the half-wall, he focused on Nate in front of the fridge. "How long was I out?"

Nate jumped about a mile, spinning around. "Jesus. A couple hours. You were zonked. I unpacked a bunch, and I was just..." He glanced behind him at the fridge. "I don't know if I'm doing it right, but I thought you'd like it. Make it feel more like home."

Lucas realized the fridge was now covered in magnets. He'd brought a big plastic container filled with his dad's collection, and now they decorated the fridge. Wrapping the duvet around him, he shuffled over, taking in the familiar images.

There was a hot-pink magnet shaped like Florida; a cheesy plastic replica of a San Francisco trolley; a Hawaiian surfer with the words "Hang ten!"; a block of cheese from Wisconsin; an old-time Coke bottle; one from the National Air and Space Museum that proclaimed, "Failure is not an option."

Lucas swallowed thickly. They were all here, out of the box and displayed where they belonged. His dad would love it. "It's..."

"Obviously you can change the order. I'm sorry. I should have let you do it."

"No. Thank you for doing this." He met Nate's worried gaze. "It's perfect." He didn't have any other words, so he kissed Nate instead and brought him back to bed.

After finishing their unpacking the next morning and getting rid of the stuff that wouldn't fit, Lucas suggested a trip down to Union Square. The square was ablaze with Christmas lights and chock full of covered wooden artisan booths, and they wandered the rows of stalls as the light drizzle turned to fat flurries. Lucas was struck with the holiday spirit. "I have an idea."

Nate lowered his camera and cocked a brow. "Does it have something to do with sex?"

"Is that *all* you think about?" Lucas huffed in mock exasperation.

Nate leaned in, his breath warm on Lucas's neck. "When you're around? Pretty much, yeah."

Despite himself, Lucas blushed and a shiver of desire coiled around his spine. "Believe me, we'll get to that later. For now, my idea involves twenty dollars and this marketplace."

"I'm listening."

"I propose we split up for half an hour and buy each other a Hanukkah present. Twenty-dollar limit."

"Shouldn't you get a Christmas present?"

"Call it a 'Chrismukkah' gift, then."

Laughing, Nate said, "Okay. Twenty dollars. Half an hour." He returned his camera to its case and glanced at the time on his phone. "Meet back here." Then he was gone, disappearing into the throng of shoppers. Nate always enjoyed a challenge.

Lucas hurried off in the other direction, examining each stall's wares. He considered a pair of supple leather gloves and wondered if he could talk the seller down. In the end he didn't even try; the thought of haggling made him faintly nauseated.

Row after row, Lucas struggled against the crowd, considering and then discarding gift ideas. Everything was either too expensive or just not right. Perhaps this game hadn't been a good suggestion after all.

A large Star of David hanging from the top of one stall caught his eye, and Lucas angled through the crowd. Just as he reached the stall, he heard Nate's chuckle from his left. Nate joined him, smiling. "Fancy meeting you here."

Lucas laughed. "Well, I asked myself, what do you get the Jew who has everything?"

"Tell me the answer isn't a Star of David wall hanging to decorate our new place."

"Not on your life." Lucas glanced at the woman operating the stall. "Um, no offense."

The young woman waved her hand. "None taken. But I'll have you know those are very popular with Staten Island ladies of a certain age." She indicated the rest of her wares. "Maybe there's something else more to your liking."

Lucas and Nate looked over the collection of novelty yarmulkes and kosher dog treats. There was also a velvet case of jewelry containing silver necklaces and bracelets with dangling stars. Another case held rings, and Nate picked up a silver ring inscribed with Hebrew, spinning it around between his fingers.

"Ah, that's a beauty," the woman said. "It says '*ani ledodi vedodi li*.' It means 'I am my beloved's, and my beloved is mine.'"

Nate held it in his palm. "How much?"

"Wait, what?" Lucas blinked in surprise.

The woman sized them up. "I'll give you two for sixty dollars. Normally eighty." She took a quick look at Lucas's hand and pulled out another ring. "Try this one."

Lucas took it from her. The silver was decent quality and the ring felt solid in his hand. He smiled uncertainly at Nate. "Um…"

"Don't worry, I'm not proposing." Nate took the ring from Lucas's hand. He slid it onto Lucas's left ring finger, where it fit perfectly.

"Could've fooled me." The butterflies unleashed in his belly flapped like crazy.

Nate grinned. "Just want to make sure it fits." He tried on his own ring, sliding it on his ring finger. It was a bit too big, so the woman gave him another size.

She smiled. "They look good on you, boys."

Lucas didn't know what to say. "Uh… Thanks." His head swam as he looked down at the ring. He knew he loved Nate with all his heart, but they'd only been together a year. "I guess we're going over the twenty-dollar limit."

"Will you throw in two chains?" Nate asked.

The woman pondered it for a moment. "You drive a hard bargain. What the heck? It's Hanukkah. Almost."

Nate took Lucas's hand and slipped the ring from his finger. "We can wear them around our necks until we're ready."

Lucas swallowed hard over the sudden lump in his throat.

Nate's smile vanished. "Shit, I totally freaked you out, didn't I? I know it's spur of the moment, and I was the one who used to be all, I don't want a boyfriend. But you changed everything, and I thought… Look, we don't have to—"

"Would you shut up? I love you, and you love me. So why not?" Lucas pressed their lips together. Turning to the beaming woman, he smiled in return. "We'll take them."

Riding the creaky elevator in their building an hour later, Lucas couldn't stop smiling. He loved the feel of the ring against his chest and knowing that Nate felt the same brush of silver. Lucas leaned in close to him. "Think I'll get lucky tonight?"

Nate caught his mouth in a kiss. "You just might. Good thing I told Mom and Dad we had too much unpacking left to make it tonight."

Guilt tugged at Lucas. "Maybe we should still go. Even if we miss the blessings and the menorah lighting, we could still see everyone. Rachel texted me a bunch of sad faces."

"The great thing about Hanukkah is that it's eight nights. We'll make sure we go to Aunt Linda's for her big dinner and gift exchange. I'm beat. I just want to curl up in our bed."

"I can't really argue with that." Lucas nuzzled Nate's cheek. "I love quiet nights."

At their apartment door, Lucas fished his keys out of his pocket, but when he twisted the knob, the door sprung open. Lucas knew his mouth was gaping, but he didn't know how else to react to the sight of what had to be Nate's entire family crammed into their tiny studio apartment.

Fifteen or so people stared back at him, some standing in the kitchen shoulder to shoulder, kids on Nate and Lucas's bed poking their heads out through the open space above the half-wall.

Lucas's first response was a flare of panic at all the people in such a small area, but at least there was no pounding bass or beer bongs being passed around. He took a long breath and blew it out slowly. It was okay. These weren't strangers. They were family.

Among the crowd, Lucas spotted Mr. and Mrs. Kramer, Nate's grandparents, Sam, Linda, and Rachel—who grinned. Lucas glanced at Nate beside him, appearing equally stunned. Nate shook his head and said, "I knew we shouldn't have given my parents the spare key."

Laughter rang out, and a few people shouted, "Surprise!" as Lucas and Nate took off their jackets and threw them on top of the overloaded coat stand behind the door.

Mrs. Kramer gave them a stern look. "Well, we had no choice when you said you weren't coming tonight. Besides, we have to give your apartment a proper housewarming and blessing."

Mr. Kramer held a blue rectangular case several inches long. Golden symbols were carved on it. He said to Lucas, "In this case is a *mezuzah*. It's a scroll of parchment with two chapters from the Torah handwritten on it and rolled very small. We hang the case on the doorpost to ask God's protection." He squeezed through the throng with a hammer and opened the door, nailing the case to the frame.

Nate's Aunt Linda recited a blessing in Hebrew, and Lucas bowed his head. When he lifted it again, through the maze of people jammed into the apartment he spotted the gleam of something in the window. Craning his head, he realized a golden menorah stood on the windowsill.

Following his gaze, Linda exclaimed, "Look at the time! The sun is almost down, and we have to light the menorah."

Nate noticed it for the first time. "You brought yours?" he asked his mother.

She smiled. "No. This is for *your* home."

Nate hugged her and pressed a kiss to her cheek. His grandfather inched his way to the menorah as people shuffled out of the way.

The old man, who always wore his yarmulke whenever Lucas saw him, smoothed it with a gnarled finger before reciting the blessings from memory.

Some of Nate's family spoke along with him, and Nate slipped his arm over Lucas's shoulder. Lucas wrapped his arm around Nate's waist, unable to wipe the smile from his face.

When Papa was finished, he pointed toward Lucas. Lucas glanced over his shoulder. "Me?"

"Yes, you. Come here and light the candles."

Nate nodded and gave him a gentle push. Lucas shimmied past the coffee table and a few of Nate's cousins, and took the long match from the old man.

"Do you know which candles to light?" Nate's grandfather peered at him with watery eyes.

Lucas felt as if he was answering the most important pop quiz of his life. "The middle one, then the candle on the far right."

The old man nodded, and Lucas exhaled and struck the match. When the candles were lit, everyone burst into applause, and after another blessing, they sang a joyous song. Nate stood next to Lucas, singing along. The new ring sat against Lucas's chest, the metal warm and solid.

Every surface in their narrow little kitchen was covered with food—latkes and sufganiyot and a dozen delicious dishes Lucas couldn't name yet. Nate's bubbe bustled around with Linda, heating everything in the oven and Lucas's old microwave.

Nate pulled out his camera and asked Rachel to take a picture of him and Lucas by the window, the menorah silhouetted by the falling snow. They stood close, and Lucas thought of how in a few hours when they were alone again, they'd sleep in each other's arms naked except for the matching rings.

In their tiny apartment in Hell's Kitchen, crammed full of family, Lucas knew he was home.

THE END

About the Author

Keira aims for the perfect mix of character, plot, and heat in her M/M romances. She writes everything from swashbuckling pirates to heartwarming holiday escapism. Her fave tropes are enemies to lovers, age gaps, forced proximity, and passionate virgins. Although she loves delicious angst along the way, Keira guarantees happy endings!

Discover more at:
KeiraAndrews.com

9 781988 260761